Briefs for the Reading Room

Micronovels for Easy Digestion

Dan Marvin
Lawrenceburg, KY USA

Published by: Marvcorp Publishing
              125 Canterbury Street
              Lawrenceburg, KY 40342

Email the author: daniel.marvin@gmail.com

ISBN: 978-0-9822783-0-7

Printed in the United States of America

Introduction – We all spend time in the bathroom. I do, the President does, the Pope does, Jennifer Aniston does, even you do I bet! Come on, admit it, you do don't you? See, it's as close to a Universal Truth as you're likely to find in this book. In fact, on average we all spend 14 years of our lives in the bathroom! OK, I made that up, but it's probably close.

Who has time to read these days? And yet, nature has provided us with the perfect opportunity to multi-task. It's quiet, we're sitting, and talking on the phone in there is… well, it's kind of gross. Really. Even texting is just… eww. But a book! A book is the perfect way to make the most of your down time.

The problem with most reading material is you have to sit through pages of plot and development and just plain writing to get to the end. Not with these stories! I don't insult your intelligence by filling in every little detail for you. Instead, I jump right to the good part, wrap it up in a hurry, and let you get on with your life. In an average sitting I bet you can read two or three of these 'micro-novels' and come away feeling well read and relieved at the same time! No need to thank me.

I've been writing these stories for years so you're getting the sum total of 20+ years of mostly silly, sometimes funny, often thoughtful experience. I'm happy to share them with you. Some other places you can read these stories are:

- At the dog park
- While getting your car washed
- While eating alone at a restaurant
- While waiting for your over-priced coffee drink to get made
- At the beach before you fall asleep and get really burned except for a rectangle on your chest where this book ended up
- In line at the bank
- While getting your hair cut
- Waiting for the idiot ahead of you to pick out his donuts, next time bring a list dude
- During the two minutes between getting anesthesia and going to sleep
- At your kids' soccer game while he's on the bench
- Any other time you can't afford to get engrossed in a full novel but want to know what happens at the end

Dedicated to: My wife, who gave me monogrammed toilet paper for our paper anniversary.

Contents

The World Under the Utility Sink

A call to arms by Dan Marvin

Magical sprites filled the air in the Kingdom of Nagale, singing beautiful songs and twinkling like a million fireflies seen through the trees. Of course, when Edgar tried to catch a few for dinner, they dissipated as if they were nothing but the wind.

Edgar had been here three days and man, was he hungry. The Leprechauns tasted like shoe leather and were about as tough and the wood nymphs squealed when you pulled their arms out until a magical princess came and yelled at you. When you went after her with a fork, she zapped you into the next county for Pete's sake! How was a guy to get three squares a day in such a rotten place?

A peal of laughter caught his attention and he saw a fairy flitting through the trees spreading pixie dust and generally being a nuisance. Surely one fairy wouldn't be missed! Edgar began to formulate a plan.

As he watched, the fairy flew closer and closer to the bush where he was hiding. His mouth began to water as it made its way to the waiting net. Would it never get here? Finally, the fairy was in range. Edgar threw the net over its head and reeled it in like a trophy bass! The fairy bit and kicked until he could get it filleted and ready to be roasted.

His fire that night held the fixings of a glorious feast. A spearmint sauce bubbled daintily on a flat rock and the fairy filled the air with the aroma of seared meat as it rotated lazily on a spit. Edgar, hungry as he was, took the time to savor every bite, stopping only long enough to die when he realized the magic mushrooms he had painstakingly sautéed were deadly poison.

The End

Fabricated Factoid:

73 - The percentage of people who feel ripped off if they come to a mostly blank page in a book.
27 - The percentage of people who are happy to find a blank page so they can take notes on what they've read
100 - The percentage of the 27% above who characterized themselves as "socially awkward" and "unpopular" in High School.

Fighting Chance

Contemporary fiction by Dan Marvin

Without the suit, he was just a man. His limbs weren't particularly strong, his eyes couldn't see around corners, he couldn't jump high or run fast or throw things a long ways. About all he could do was sit in his recliner and think back to how it had been.

Back in the day, "Do Good Man" was a household name. Whenever a seemingly unstoppable force of evil would come to town, he got the call. He had a direct line to the Commissioners Office and it used to ring off the hook. Not these days. There were no calls for "Ordinary Man." There were lots of ordinary men on the payroll that were just fine jumping in and grabbing the headlines when the menace was tame.

For awhile, the headlines had screamed for him. "Super Huge Eel Swallows Aquarium, Who Will Save Us?" Then a strange thing happened. With no one to fight them, the super villains simply moved on. It seemed that the adrenaline rush was half the fun and no one actually wanted to run this moribund little backwoods Metropolis. They moved on to bigger fish, so to speak, and he was no longer "Do Good Man", he was just "Man." All because of the suit.

With a sigh, he drained his beer and looked for a rerun of Seinfeld. It wasn't as funny to him anymore. Once he knew he could easily defeat the Soup Nazi and win a cup of his delicious soup. Now, he didn't even know if he could match wits with Newman. He seriously wondered if he needed some Abilify. That stuff seemed awesome in the commercials. Even the dogs perked up.

Lost in his own thoughts, he barely heard the doorbell, it didn't even register. When it rang again, it intruded into his brain enough that he realized that… someone wanted him. He was wanted! He sprang from his chair and ran to the door.

"Sign here for your suit," said the man from the drycleaners. "Sorry it took so long, it had some acid stains and we had to send it to Cleveland to get them out." Eagerly he signed for his suit, tipped the disinterested delivery man, and streaked for his bedroom.

With shaking hands, he opened the plastic garment bag and realized he had been given Gopher Woman's suit by mistake. Collapsing onto the bed, Do Good Man wept.

The End

Dubious Definition – Arsenal (n) – a bad place to store your nal

A Victim of Circumstance

Nail biting suspense from Dan Marvin who has been compared to Alfred Hitchcock, albeit unfavorably.

It was almost noon. I could tell by the clock on the wall, it pointed to different numbers that told my brain that it was almost noon. Plus my stomach was growling. You know how it is. I had just decided to go down to the Grimy Deli for a $5 plate of heartburn when Lila stuck her head in my door with a message. That's where she's talked to someone and they've asked her to tell me something. I get them all the time, everyone does, they're messages, like I said.

This one was different. It didn't contain any words in the same order that I recognized from previous messages, that's what made it unique. It was the kind of message that tells me something completely new, something I wouldn't have known if I didn't see it. It was that kind of message. My Private Eye instincts kicked into overdrive because I'm a private dick, a finder of things that people want found. I locate people and information that would have gone unlocated if it weren't for me and therefore have good instincts. Like I said, a Private Eye.

"Watch out. A large object is about to fall on you." That's what the message said. It might have been code, that's where somebody tells you something that isn't what it appears. If you're smart enough, you can figure out what it's actually supposed to say. Pretty clever, if you ask me. It seemed like it might have been code.

I studied the message Lila had given me. It was printed on a "Here's your Message" Post It note, the kind that one comes off the top and it sticks to stuff but not too tight because you will want to throw it out eventually. You know the type. It looked familiar, much like the paper Lila usually uses to give me messages. That was it! It was a message from Lila, the kind I usually got! Now we were getting somewhere. That's where you are arriving at a place different from where you were earlier.

Now that I was on the right track, I happened to glance up. Actually, it was more of a reflex action that anyone would have to a large object hurtling through the air under the acceleration of gravity and crashing through the roof above you. You put 100 people in a room with a large object crashing down on top of them and all 100 would look up, I guarantee it! The note started to make sense now. I could tell it was...

The End

A Posse of One

A story of love and redemption by Dan Marvin

Over the next ridge lay water. Ladstone knew it, he just had to convince his tired horse and his sun swollen eyes to find it. They had been riding two days, hard and long. The meager provisions he had been able to steal from the stable hand barely lasted a day and the water had been used mainly for the mangy dapple he was riding with little for himself.

Only 72 hours separated him from the life of a wayward but very successful gambler. A bad night, some bad hombres, and suddenly he was running for his life, all that he had built gone. In a way, it was fitting. All that he had built was on the backs of businessmen and cattlemen and farmers, all of whom needed the money more than he. Still, it was a suitable life for a man of refined tastes and he missed it acutely at this very moment.

Ladstone crested the ridge and saw more of the same, unremarkable scrub and sun-beaten earth. With a grimace, he gritted his teeth and slapped the reins. The dapple started off resolute but exhausted. If he didn't find water soon, both he and the horse would be dead.

The ridge allowed him to scan the country behind him. At least there were no tell-tale columns of dust to be seen. Either his pursuers had lost interest or were very good at what they did. A small copse of trees lay ahead.

Although the patch of trees didn't look very inviting, they were all he had. He crawled on his belly under the scrub brush and prickers until he happened on earth that looked like it might have been wet sometime in the last several months. With his hands and a broken branch, he carved out a hole in the center. Ever so slowly, it began to fill with brackish, brown water. The first hatful went to the horse. Then, Ladstone allowed himself to drink. He gulped the water and bathed his head.

This would have to do for the night. He set up a meager camp, set up a snare for any wayward wildlife, and rested. The horse nibbled on some forlorn looking grass a few feet away. He wouldn't be going anywhere. The sun began to set and Ladstone began to relax. A few feet away, a small explosion set the earth falling over him. Ducking for cover in the briars, Ladstone waited.

Nothing moved. The earth was as quiet as if all life had long ago died out and it was now waiting for him to do the same. After what seemed like an eternity, Ladstone went to investigate. A large rock, blackened and melted sat in the center of the small crater. A meteorite had almost vaporized him!

Years later, as a successful businessman in Austin, it defied odds that Ladstone was actually killed by another meteor. The heavens really had it in for him.

The End

Beware the Ides of 2179

Contemporary fiction by Dan Marvin

In the swirling mists of mid day, the mining colony looked like a handful of jacks on a dusty playground. Sitting in the driver's seat of the cruiser, Mac McWain perused the desolate landscape he called home. Twelve years ago, he had accepted a short assignment as project specialist for a mining colony. That had been before they even knew about the Veegon.

The Veegon had struck mercilessly at the fledgling outposts of new space-power earth. Alpha Zed 3 (AZ3) was the last mining colony and one of only seven outposts to survive at all. Through a hurried alliance with the Grinls, they had survived the onslaught. Now, they had to pay them back in precious ores and minerals (PO&M).

Mac's short assignment had turned into a lifelong pursuit. Earth Central (EC) wouldn't waste space on a freight ship for a person even if they were inclined to let him leave. Mac was resigned to his fate, and his bones were slowly wasting away, leaving him unfit to return anyway.

There was a bright spot to all this. He had complete autonomy from earth. Any messages for him were days getting here on pulsed light relay (PLR) and by that time, whatever was important then most likely wasn't now. There was food, water, shelter, and even a girl he kinda liked. The thought of Mafan sent blood rushing to his face.

Mac broke out of his reverie and continued on his mission, to transport core samples to the testing lab for a full analysis spread (FAS). The ore veins they had been working in the area had begun to play out and he desperately needed to find a new source to keep the shipments flowing. The color of these looked promising.

At Airlock 7, the vehicle was de ionized and he pulled it into a refueling bin. He hailed an Automatic Conveyance Device (ACD) to cart the samples to the lab and headed to his quarters for a quick shower. The lab results would be slow coming; he should have time for a bite to eat and a pint of Alpha Orbital Ale (AOA).

A rumbling in the personnel transport tube (PTT) warned him that something was amiss. A Huge Alation Stone Worm (HASW) burst from the surface awakened from his centuries long slumber (CLS) by the drilling equipment and quickly ate everything in sight (AEIS).

The End

20,000 Leagues of Their Own

A romantic tale of warfare at sea by Dan Marvin

A gentle vibration indicated that the engines had engaged and the surreal undersea view started to move. Captain Durain looked around the cabin and read the nervous tension on the faces of his crew. As quietly as possible, the *Spirit of Hoboken* moved out, hoping to avoid detection by the enemy topside.

She leaked a bit of oil into the turgid water but seemed to have weathered the depth charges well. The backup generators kicked off and primary power returned, indicating the Chief Engineer had somewhat overstated the lead time required to redirect the output into the secondary wiring harness. In all, they could have been much worse off.

Under the blanket of static the jammers provided, they might have a snowball's chance in hell of getting clear of the destroyer above and radioing for help. Might. Still, it was impossible to disband the knots in his stomach waiting for the next depth charge to detonate. Ahead, the outlines of a large cavern began to unfold. Captain Durain formulated a quick change of strategy.

In the war room of the *USS Dole*, Durain's counterpart was getting red in the face. "What do you mean we LOST them?!" he demanded, incredulous. "They were dead in the water, powerless and adrift! How did we just LOSE them?" A string of technobabble from the sonar operator indicated that he didn't know. "Find them!" Captain Desmont yelled as he stormed out. The *Dole* began to look in earnest.

The forlorn 'ping' of active sonar went over their head 8 times in the next 6 hours. The destroyer must have been circling in an ever widening sweep to track them down. Durain's crew could not afford a cough, a whisper, or a thump to give them away. The strain was overwhelming.

Suddenly, the sonar was joined with another sound, the muffled explosion of depth charges. They were far away but ominous, searching for a target but finding only fish. Still, the *Spirit of Hoboken* waited silently.

A gentle rocking indicated that all was not well for the submarine. Was this cavern seismically active? Durain could not afford to find out. He ordered full astern and the engines engaged once more. As the sub began to move, the cavern began to close. The centuries old slumbers of the colossal sea eel had ended with the depth charges and it engulfed the submarine on the way to the surface. Once there, it added the destroyer to its lunch.

Captain Durain hoped fervently that the colossal sea eel had a quick metabolism.

Unfortunately for Captain Durain not…

The End

Functionally Literate - The Idaho Deming Story

Biographical nonsense by Dan Marvin

By the time he was just 17, Jacob Brawn had been a prospector, a gambler, a cowpuncher, and was rapidly getting the reputation of being a hard man in a hard land. His fists were legendary, his temper was volatile, and he drank straight whiskey from sun up to sun down.

Marian Bronson was a demure young woman, good Western stock and the apple of her father's eye, the rancher Rocky Bronson. Her mother had died in an Indian fight years ago and he had raised her, spoiling her with everything she wanted. Despite the temptation, she had been relatively good and saved her best tears for very big ticket items.

When the cocky young man rode into the ranch yard, Marian stood behind the curtains of the sitting room and watched him. He was quite a sight, rippling muscles could barely be contained by his shirt, his eyes held fire and laughter. Her father sauntered out to meet him.

"Howdy, sir..." Jacob began. "Race Johnson at the stable said you might be looking for some help. I may be young but I've roped and ridden plenty of miles." Rocky had heard of Jacob's reputation and was wary. With some quick negotiation, they decided to give each other a try. Jacob Brawn's eye was caught by a flutter of cloth at the window as he turned.

Marion turned from the pane of glass that had separated her from the fine young man. She knew in her heart that they would meet. She also knew that she must have him. Jacob was blissfully unaware of his fate.

Many years later, as he brought in groceries, listening to his wife nag him about his lack of earning potential on a Saturday night while his friends were at the Lurchin' Lizard saloon, Jacob secretly prayed for death.

Not, unfortunately for Jacob, The End

Questionable Quotation – "Ask not what your country can do for you because quite frankly, we're about out of ideas." - FDR

If you love something...

A play in three acts by Dan Marvin

Halfway through his dinner, Dinardo sat upright and stared at his companion. "What did you say?" He snarled with disbelief. Mabel Anne shrunk back into her seat and sat motionless, afraid lest she reawaken his anger. He had been so much better lately, the last thing she wanted to do was piss him off.

For now, he let the transgression slide and returned to his beef. The minutes ticked away in silence. Dinardo's brow softened, Mabel could almost see the working of his mind. "I'm sorry I snapped. Please, finish what you were saying."

Heartened, she returned to her narrative. "I want to go back to school. I've always wanted to finish my degree." She looked at him from under her eyebrows to watch his reaction.

"I see." The veins on Dinardo's neck were sticking out. To his credit, he paused before he continued. "If that is your dream, let's see what we need to do to get you enrolled." As far as he was concerned, the topic was closed. Mabel Anne gave him a happy kiss. "Thank you! I'm so happy. I want to be productive again. Raising the children was rewarding, but now that they're gone..."

"I said you could, now let me finish my meal, woman" he grumbled. Deep down, she knew he loved her. There had been a time in his life when the anger owned him. With lots of help and support, he owned it most of the time now.

Fifteen months later, Mabel Anne walked across the stage to accept her diploma. She tipped her cap for the audience to see. Some laughed; others wondered what the message meant. It said "so long, sucker." She jumped in the Buick and headed to Vegas. Dinardo would never see her again.

The End

Pharcical Philosophy – Humans have, like 500 bones or something in their hands, but only one covering their head so it's no wonder we tend to be pretty inflexible in our thinking.

Happenstance

Contemporary fiction by Dan Marvin

The attic creaked above him, weight from unknown footsteps forcing reluctant groans from the ancient rafters. The air in the house was cold, unnaturally cold, even though the temperature outside hovered close to 85, inside it couldn't have been more than 50 degrees. He pulled his light jacket around him and shivered, hoping the noises would stop. They didn't.

Jeffry had stopped by that morning on a whim, tempted by the Bobby's childish goading and his own curiosity. After the Martins had been murdered three years ago, the house had quickly been boarded up and no one had been in it since to his knowledge. There were stories of night-time apparitions and weird wailings in the night; everyone knew that it had to be the Martin's ghosts, unable to sleep eternally until their killers had been brought to justice. Jeffry wanted to help set them free.

He had begun by going around to the back of the house, checking the boards on the cellar windows. It quickly became evident that he wasn't the first kid with this idea. One of the boards was loose and could be swung rather easily out of the way revealing a broken window that led into the cellar. He climbed through, shining his flashlight around him even though the other windows let in some scant light.

The cellar was mostly empty. There were some beer cans and other garbage that stood testament to the perseverance of young people looking for somewhere to make less attractive in the guise of "partying." He knew that someday he'd understand the allure; he couldn't wait to get old enough to be cool. This was the first step, just wait until the kids at school heard that he went into the Martin place.

As Jeffery snooped around the house, he didn't notice that the once sunny day had started to cloud over. A late spring breeze sprang up and blew in some clouds that began to darken and thicken. Soon, it was sprinkling; he did hear the sound on the windows. He knew that he was going to have to wait here for the shower to pass; they were always over in an hour or so. The door to the upstairs yawned open and he began to ascend.

Halfway up the stairs, a draft from somewhere blew the door shut. He sprinted the remaining stairs, panting and out of breath as he got to the top. He looked down into the staircase; sure he would see a ghost materialize out of the ether, looking to do him grievous bodily injury. Instead, he saw some stairs and a closed door. He began to search the bedrooms.

In the second bedroom there was still some furniture. From a crack between the boards, he saw the wind and rain lash against the house; this was a particularly nasty storm. Jeffry began to rethink how good an idea this actually was. As he sat, waiting out the storm, comforted by a room with some actual furniture, he heard the moaning. It could be wind in the eves, or it could be Mr. Anderson looking for him. Jeffry shivered.

He curled up into as compact a ball as he could, sitting in the overstuffed chair that the mice had started to systematically disassemble. The wailing from overhead was joined by the obligatory banging and the creaking of the joists above him. Jeffry was terrified as the bedroom door opened and...

"Jeffry, it's time for lunch. Why are you in your closet?" His mother handed him a ham sandwich. He'd have to wait for another day to be cool.

The End

Erroneous Excerpt – "... then through the trees did slant light, bright and bold and in such intensity that I had to avert my eyes. Almost blinded, I placed my hand over my eyes to see from whence it derived, to find only darkness again. Thoroughly creeped out, I sprang from Walden grabbing up only what essentials I might in the midst of unreasoning panic. Armed thus with a doily and a chamber pot, I made my way into the night never to return to my cabin on the pond..."

Escape from Walden – Ralph Waldo Thoreau

Telefurbies

Contemporary fiction by Dan Marvin

He picked up the telephone and began to dial, methodically. It was his job. The phone rang once, then twice, then a voice, pleasant but cautious. He knew before he even spoke that soon he would be dialing again. "Hello, have I reached Mrs. Richardson?" The phone went dead without even an 'I'm not interested.' Richard crossed the name off the list and moved one spot down.

The ring on the phone was old fashioned, a buzz and not a nice modern ring. The connection ratched at him once, then twice, and then there was a voice. A tiny "hello?" greeted his ear. He sighed.

"Hi sweetie, is your mommy or daddy home?" Richard tried his best to keep his voice sugary sweet and happy. He hated kids. Oddly, the voice on the other end of the line started... crying. This was new. "Are you OK honey?" He asked, wondering what he had gotten into.

"Daddy is here" he heard the child say, "but mommy is sick, at least that's what daddy told me. He told me not to come in there but I saw mommy on the floor and he was all red." The line was quiet except for her silent sobs. Richard sat back, dazed.

"What do you mean he was all red?" he asked, trying to decide if this was a real emergency.

"He was all red, and so was mommy. He sounded funny. Mommy wouldn't move. Then he told me to go play. I'm scared." The crying sounded in the background again. Richard thought quickly to himself. He was just a telemarketer for God's sake! Still, he put the girl on hold and called 911.

"Hello, this is Richard Thomas. I need you to trace this phone number (he gave the number). I think there has been some sort of accident there." Richard gave details for a few more moments and then the operator told him to keep the girl talking. He sighed and hung up, then switched back to the other phone.

"Honey, are you there?" He asked. The line was very quiet. Suddenly, a new voice answered.

"Who is this?" The man's voice was gruff and strident, but filled with strain. Richard didn't know whether to answer or hang up. He decided to answer, to give the girl a chance.

"My name is Richard. Is everything all right there?" He didn't know how to keep the man on the line, his mind raced.

"Sure everything is all right, who is this?" In the background, Richard could hear the man telling the little girl to please, please quit crying, daddy was on the phone. At least she was still OK. Suddenly, the sound of sirens could be heard. The man was back on the line. "I've got caller ID Mr... Thomas. You've just made a big mistake!" The phone went dead.

Richard Thomas sat back, dripping with sweat. He was just a telemarketer! After a moment he picked up the phone, looked at the list, looked at the phone, and carefully set it back down. He stood up and walked out the door.

Rainbow Roy and the River Raiders

A tale from America's Old West by Dan Marvin

Rainbow Roy swooped his horse "Dusty" down the slope and towards the banks of the river below. He had followed the Copper boys down to their hideout and now was getting ready to round 'em up, one way or another. Old man Copper and his oldest son Colt were the ringleaders of the gang and they had been raising Hell all up and down the river valley. Now, Rainbow Roy (who was a Ranger) was ready to take them to justice. It was his job to put an end to their antics and the government had given him the power to do it in whatever way he wanted or needed to.

He pulled at the reins and dismounted from Dusty, the faithful steed, tying him to a tree and preparing to go the rest of the way on foot. He crept slowly up on the small cabin nestled in the clearing and peered cautiously into the window which was slightly ajar.

"Colt," the old man was saying, "what is the nature of the universe?"

"The ancient Greeks had one way of looking at it dad..." Colt started but suddenly there was a commotion from the other room. The rest of the gang had been playing Bocce Ball and now someone had been caught cheating. Syringes were drawn and things looked bad.

Now was Roy's chance! He leaped through the window and shouted "hands up!" as he sailed through the air. Everyone was taken very much by surprise as they were all thoroughly engrossed in the action in the other room. The syringes were dropped and everyone started to come peacefully. Colt Copper, in a desperate final move, drew a hideout potato peeler and ran towards Roy. In a quick karate type move, Roy disarmed Colt and grabbed him by the neck.

Several miles upstream, the dam collapsed and the valley was flooded. Days later, the bloated, decomposing body of Dusty washed up on the shores of Goldtown, the last reminder of that great Ranger, Rainbow Roy.
(Western music builds and fades, break to commercial)

The End

Author's Note – Seriously, this isn't too much blank space, do you really think I should have to fill it?

Two Days in Paradise

Multi-cultural fiction by Dan Marvin

The third Tuesday after the sunfruit harvest was the traditional Festival of Zambir. Throughout the island, wives were busy fermenting the sunfruit into sloof and the children braided each other's hair with bits of shell and bright fabrics. Chief Rafeesh looked out from his hut and inhaled the pungent odor of sloof, smiling broadly as he thought of the festival just two days away. He had much to do!

He bowed deep at the altar of the sea god, and then walked down the hill to the beach. The trees spoke to him, the muted whisperings of his ancestors. He smiled at their familiar quarrel, whether to whirl this way or that, until finally they were out of his hearing. The sun greeted him warmly, reflecting from the ocean waves and the brilliant white sand. He sang the joyous Hymn of the Morning and swam to the sandbar and back to cleanse away yesterday's woes leaving him more room to enjoy today's delights.

Miya had his breakfast ready when he returned and they ate robustly of eggs and fruits, gathered from the forest around them. Dried fish from two days before added an interesting flavor to the repast and he complimented her on its preparation. "I am lucky indeed to be honored with your love. I thank the sea god for this providence." Miya blushed slightly and went about cleaning up the eating area.

Enjoying a pipe of Tumanj at the door, he could see the village below as it began to bustle to life. So much to do! So much to prepare! The wet season would soon be upon them and it was time to enjoy the fruits of this seasons harvest with good friends and merriment. He saw the Krajoc the man of medicine approaching and prepared to receive his friend. Krajoc was getting old, but every morning he braved the hill to give Rafeesh counsel. It was good.

"Krajoc my friend! Will you join me in Tumanj?" Rafeesh offered him a seat and the pipe. Krajoc lifted it to his lips and inhaled deeply, welcoming the rush as he had on countless mornings before. Together they sat that way for quite some time, the sound of the ocean waves filling the silence between old friends. Krajoc had counseled Rafeesh for years, and his father Rutibee before him and he trusted the man completely. His hair was white and his legs bent but his wise eyes still held the intensity of a man half his age.

"Rafeesh, we must speak of Zambir," Krajoc said after the Tumanj was spent and the hour grew late. "I predict the weather will turn sour this year. We must decide if the festival should go on as planned." They bundled their heads closer and talked of the pros and cons of canceling the festival. Rafeesh had no doubt that the weather would turn. Inside the hut, Miya fretted. She had been working so hard to make the best sloof she had ever made; it would be a shame not to drink it.

Finally, with much chagrin, Chief Rafeesh decided. This year, the festival would be called on account of weather. He and Krajoc set out down the mountain to tell the others. There would be much disappointment but storms brewed swiftly and all would need their senses if one descended upon them when they were involved in the festival.

Zambir day dawned bright and beautiful; the sun spoke to him as usual as Chief Rafeesh swam out to the sandbar. One hour turned to two which turned to four, but there was no sign of the storm. Rafeesh decided to seek out Krajoc who had broken his morning ritual and stayed away this morning. When he got to Krajoc's hut, he was really pissed to find the medicine man tanked on sloof.

The End

Fabricated Factoid –

15 – Percentage of people who believe everything they read
85 – Percentage of people who won't believe that 15% of everyone else believes everything they read.

Two Summers Tales

A moral dilemma from Dan Marvin

The heat wafted up from the pavement like a living thing, the ghost with all the sparkles in it from Star Trek maybe... it hinted at vast vistas of greenery ahead but all the hints I'd had in the last two hundred miles had yielded a lot more nothing. The car wasn't really too bad, the A/C still seemed interested in keeping me cool and I had a decent supply of bottled water on hand. The gas gauge read 3/4's and the map showed at least three more well baked towns between me and the border. Most importantly, no signs of blue and red lights coming up behind me, hoping to stop my forward progress.

It had all started last summer with a casual conversation around the table at the cottage after a few two many tequila shots and a few too few job interviews. Benny was a compelling public speaker, and he decided to turn on the charm right away, making the idea far more likely sounding than it should have. "There's this really big safe at work and it's full of money." A conversation that starts like that makes you sit up and pay attention, even with a few two many tequila shots eating away at your guts.

I'd never considered myself a master criminal, my idea of illegal was going 64 in a 55. Still, there was a certain amount of appeal to one night's work and a lifetime of not having to worry if I had turned off the fryer before I left. Just try getting that one off your record, I dare ya. One boneheaded move and you're branded for life. So, as Benny started spinning his fantasy, I began taking notes, first mentally, then on the back of a napkin.

The whole thing seemed pretty easy. Securitech was a global concern based in our town. There were two entrances to the building and the safe was open during the work day. Most importantly, the guards weren't armed. They also took a break at 10AM together; both of them evidently preferred the company of the Marlboro man to that of their fellow employees. If everything went according to plan, they wouldn't even suspect us until we'd pretty much cleaned them out. Benny pushed the broom and could go anywhere, and I knew how to drive.

That was the plan, anyway. Snatch and run, no one gets hurt. It didn't really work out very well though. Benny got sick around Christmas time and ended up having his leg amputated. I got to thinking about it but couldn't figure out a way to pull it off from the outside, without him there being able to go anywhere he wanted, our plan was sunk. He wasn't doing real well on his recovery either. I noticed a lot of bedsores starting to form because his HMO apparently didn't pay to have patients turned in bed.

As I drove down the road now, heading out of the country with a big duffel bag stuffed with money and not a second to lose, the events of the last couple of weeks were front and foremost on my mind. Had I done the right thing? Was there any justification for taking money from a big company that wouldn't miss it? Would I be able to enjoy it?

Benny's eyes haunted me, the way he followed me with them as I came in to his hospital room. I remember the ping of the ventilator as it forced air down his lungs, the unnatural sucking noise as it pulled it back out again. I remember the feeling of the pillow in my hands, the pleading look in his eyes when he figured out what I was going to do. Getting an insurance policy on each other had seemed like such a good idea at the time, my guess is that Benny's last thoughts were to regret the decision...

The End

Phabricated Philosophy – Time goes quickly when you're having fun. Therefore, to live a really long life, you should never have any fun. So stop reading this book and go eat Brussels sprouts or something.

Kaidarro

An epic saga by Dan Marvin

The ocean broke upon the bow of Mandukot's ship and continued on its never-ending quest, much like the man above. He knew these seas, he had grown up here and sailed these waters with his father, the great mariner. Now he had returned, to stake his claim as the rightful heir to the throne, lord of a watery domain bordered by enemies, peopled with rebels, and filled with the riches of the seven seas.

Mandukot had traveled far, his ship was no stranger to the Far East and her bow was laden with silk. Too, he had seen the wonders of the Dark Continent, and figures of ivory took their place next to the cloth. A message hastened him back, the king lay dying, and it was time for him to return to the land of Kaidarro. He hoped his learning was complete, there was no more time.

Herlim had remained at his elbow the entire voyage. Schooled in the ways of the sea, knowledgeable of magic and man, his was the job of teacher, friend, and conscience. More than once he had saved Mandukot's life. More than once, the favor had been repaid until it sometimes seemed as though they were cut from the same cloth and of one mind. He longed for the return as much as Mandukot. He too, was ready for the challenges ahead.

A cry went up from the harbor gates, they had been spotted and were being welcomed, or so they hoped. The voices sounded excited, it was difficult to determine if from love or hate. A gate opened, and they turned their rudder towards the gap. It was time to fathom the mood of the kingdom.

It was obvious the village elders had been summoned; they stood in wait as the ship drew near. A few pleasantries said that all was well, but there was no time to waste. With a solemn procession, Mandukot and Herlim traveled to the castle walls to determine the condition of King Safrone. The massive doors opened to reveal their secrets and the travelers entered within.

"Father" Mandukot began as he entered the room. "I have returned! I received your message and I have ended my travels!" His voice boomed as he finished, his excitement at being home overwhelming his concern for his king.

"I'm afraid I was a bit premature. It was just a cold, sniffles really. I should be able to be king for quite awhile yet. Why don't you get some soup in the kitchen and stop round again in a year or so." With that, the old man rolled over and went back to sleep.

Mandukot's wild mane billowed in the wind as the salt air touched his face once more. Even though he looked quite impressive, he still felt a wee bit silly.

The End

Ernie's Wife

A story of make believe by Dan Marvin

Another gray, dismal day and Ernie set off for work. His wife had packed him a lunch (probably tuna again. It was always tuna) and sent him on his way. Ernie hoped he had remembered everything. He usually didn't. The boss would probably threaten to fire him again as he usually did and with his luck; today the boss probably would go through with it. He sniffled and wondered how long the cold would hold off. Another two days, tops. The bus jerked to a stop and Ernie got out with a look of resignation. "Only 8 hours," he thought "and then I get to go home and argue with Her until we go to bed. What a wonderful life."

As Ernie was walking into the building, the sun burst from behind the clouds and he noticed a painting in the lobby. The painting usually looked bleak and barren. Today, the sun glinted from the odd color combinations and gave it a certain charm. Ernie smiled.

"Good morning Mr. Nesmith" called his secretary cheerfully. Usually she just growled out a greeting when she said anything at all. "Would you care for some coffee?" Unprecedented!

"Nesmith, get in here!" the boss was yelling over the intercom. Great, it was starting already. "Your work on the Harrison account was inspiring. Another effort like that and you'll get that raise you've been wanting. What was this? Ernie felt faint.

He went back to his office and plowed through his work. Before he knew it, it was lunch time. Another surprise met him as his wife had packed a tasty shrimp cocktail and homemade cake. The rest of the day glided by without a hitch and Ernie got onto the bus in high spirits. He arrived home and saw all of the lights were dim. She must have gone shopping. No dinner for him tonight. Unless he cooked it himself of course. He knew it had been too good to last.

As he opened the door, he saw his wife standing there scantily clad in a sleek negligee and holding a rose in one hand with a glass of wine in the other. After a romantic dinner, they settled in to watch the football game she had taped for him and she handed him a beer. Her whispered voice in his ear promised more than just beer and football tonight... Then Ernie woke up. 6am, time to go to work.

The End

Your Money, Your Choice

A hard hitting expose by Dan Marvin

In the rollicking halls of Southside High, Ephram did not fit in. He was bit too angular and spare to hang out with the jocks, not quite smart enough to be a nerd, and ever-so-slightly too masculine to be a cheerleader. He was quiet but with a tendency to spaz out every once in awhile. His peers voted him "Most Likely to Commit Heinous Crimes Against Society" in the yearbook. To Ephram, it was an unnecessary reminder that kids can be cruel.

On this particular day, 12 days before finals week, Ephram found himself in the principal's office, his academic life hanging in the balance. As it turns out, the school had a policy against stealing girls' underwear from the locker room and wearing it as a headband. Perhaps more distressing, his lack of familiarity with the statute did not seem to be an adequate defense against the charge.

"Mr. Potts, why exactly did you abscond with the clothing articles in question?" Principal Nixon asked him.

"The voices in my head told me to," one of Ephram's personalities responded. He was quite surprised to hear the words come out of his mouth; the others usually let him do the talking. All the same, it was probably as lucid an argument as he was likely to muster.

Apparently satisfied with his soul-searching, Principal Nixon let Ephram stay at the school and even allowed him a few days of Nintendo at home as a reward. The court imposed restraining order was nice enough to give him some guidelines on proper behavior when he found himself in the girl's locker room. Yet, even with all of this resolution, the incident was to stay with Ephram for many years to come.

E. Justin "Rocky" Potts' thoughts returned to the present. Those days seemed so long ago, he had to chuckle a bit. As overseas mission leader for the marines, he rarely took the time to look back to his somewhat messy childhood. As he led his forces into what the history books would refer to as the "Really Big Battle that the Good Guys Won", General Potts was glad he had worn his lucky panties.

The End

Questionable Quotation – "Two wrongs don't make a right. But three lefts do."
-Anonymous

The Doolian Dilemma

An exploration of the super natural by Dan Marvin

With a dramatic wave of his hands, Grand Maestro Azar elevated his pretty assistant and began to move her around the room. With squeals of delight, her body hovered over the crowded hotel showroom and with equal ease; he brought her back and set her once more on the table. High above, the winches and gears groaned a bit but they were droned out by the thunderous applause of drunken retirees.

The glamorous life of an entertainer had once appealed the Herb (AKA Grand Maestro Azar), now it merely paid the bills. The suckers who wanted to be tricked had left him somewhat jaded to the wonder of his profession. His illusions were pretty to behold but lacked the force of will which could have made him the best.

On the street outside the hotel, Herb hailed a hooker and spent a goodly portion of the evening hiding various parts of his anatomy. Although his urges were sated, his mind was left unsatisfied, longing for meaning. Fate had an interesting plan for him.

In the audience that night was a woman that Herb noticed right off. It had been a long time since he had been attracted to an audience member. She seemed a bit haughty, and didn't clap as freely or as long as the others. Still, whenever he glanced her way, her piercing eyes were seeing to his soul. He was smitten.

After the show, he delayed a reasonable amount of time and then went in search of the woman he had seen. His slight psychic touch led him immediately to the hotel bar. "What kept you so long?" She asked when he was about to introduce himself. There was magic in the air that night.

The next morning, Herb awoke at peace with the world. He rolled over to say good morning to the empty air. Incredulous, he looked at the pillow that had once supported the woman from last night, what was her name? It now had only a note, "thanks for reaching into your bag of Tricks. -S"

Azar the Incensed seized Herb's mind. With the forces of magic at his disposal, he turned the pillow into a pile of feathers and shredded cloth.

The End

This space left intentionally blank.

Semi-Precious Glue

A brewing controversy by Dan Marvin

It started many years ago at a small village in the hills when the inhabitants started brewing the world's finest beer. People would trek from miles around to sip some of the precious nectar at the local watering hole "The Pitchers Bottom" and many a tale of wonder and delight passed from the lips of patrons there from far flung corners of the earth. The word of this delightful brew spread far and wide and eventually fell on the ears of evil "Orgar the Semi-Intelligent" the token force of evil on this planet. He began to crave this beer and set up a plan to get a never ending supply.

One day, at the Pitcher's Bottom, an old man in a tattered cape sat down at a table and waited patiently until the over worked waitress could take his order . As there was nothing else at the bar, the old man ordered beer and settled down to wait for its arrival. Several well meaning locals came by to see if he could be coaxed into conversation but he shooed them away with a swish of his hand. Some malignant sparkle glittered in his eye that warned off any others who would wish to mar his privacy.

Beneath his cape, the old man's visage seemed to contort and change. Those watching from nearby could see his watery blue eyes change to almost black, his stooped shoulders straighten and gain mass, and his bent back became upright before their eyes.

When his beer arrived, he sprang from his chair and threw off his cape. It was Orgar! "Where is the owner? I have a little deal for him!" He laughed at his own evil tone and the owner scurried quickly out from behind the bar.

"Y-yes," he stammered "how may I help you?"

"I want twenty kegs of this brew delivered to me every week or I shall wreak havoc upon your town and your persons!" Orgar called out impressively.

"We only brew 10 per week." Offered the timid bar owner.

"Not enough! Let all the beer here be turned to glue!" and he waved his arms in an overly dramatic way. Of course, he was not a magician and was only semi-intelligent at best so nothing happened and the villagers pummeled him for threatening their beer supply. Beer is a mighty motivator.

The End

Historically Innacurate – In 1866, Elisha Gray invented the five pack of beer but was just behind Joe Sixpack at the patent office.

Twice Around

Fiction about fiction by Dan Marvin

Mary Kate had grown up a lonely girl, the only child of two married strangers who lived in the country. Unlike in the movies, she didn't love animals, no birds landed on her outstretched finger when she whistled. Bugs bugged her and mice made her run back to her room where she would slam the door and lose herself in one of her carefully hoarded books. It was those books that took her to far away places, lost islands, abandoned mines, romantic castles set on a hill. It was the books that were her salvation, perhaps, but it was the books that kept her world wanting, not living up to the hype.

It was natural, I suppose, that Mary Kate would gravitate towards being a librarian, and she did. She was an excellent librarian in fact, prone to speaking softly and suggesting that you do so as well. She could give you a pretty good starting point on almost any topic without flipping through the card catalog. She could also make it clear that there was a wall protecting her thoughts, you were privy only to the information that she was doling out on the effects of meteor bombardments on the moon or the movements of Napoleon's army, but never to how her day was going or if she'd had a good weekend.

The books were her wings and her prison. In them she found friends that she couldn't bare to leave. The years rolled on. One day, as she was sitting in the library, cataloging the latest crop of romance novels, a novel thing happened. He walked in to the office and into her heart, a giant of a man with a soft voice and hard features. His hands were rough from hard work but his eye was clear and his questions smart. He was looking, he said, for information on his family's house. He lived but a mile from where Mary Kate's parents lived, where SHE lived too, in a house that she passed every day on the way to work. His name was Max and he thought the house had been built in the 1850's by a family named Nelson.

They pored over the documents together, two heads bent on a common mission. The microfiche projector nearly smoked from page after page, no mention of a new house going up out by Cooper's Creek, no mention of a family of Nelson's who were thinking of building. 1850 flew by, 1851 followed in it's wake, '52 and '53 went by as well, the Gazette giving little hope that Max was going to find his heritage. Then, in 1859, after several hours of 'accidentally' touching hands... there it was! "A new house was finished today by Clarence Nelson. He'll live there with his wife too. The house sits on the site of the Osgood place that burned down last year." She was frankly amazed that they had found it, and slightly disappointed that he would leave now. Then he surprised her.

The request for a cup of coffee was shy but sincere; she nodded her head in spite of her initial reaction to run out of the library. Soon they were sitting in the diner, laughing like old friends. The next day was dinner out, then a movie, then sitting at Max's 1859 house holding hands in front of the television. From there, she felt hands on her breasts and she gave into the sensation. The hands were replaced with other parts and she floated away on a river of desire...

The clock at the desk struck 6, the library was closing. Mary Kate closed Max up and slid him onto the shelf with the rest of the men she would never know. Deliberately, she stood up, composed herself, and headed home.

The End

Questionable Quotation – "Veni, Vidi, Vici, Vera Violet Vinn is very very very awful on her violin" - Julius Suess

Sunset over Shanghai

Dark gray waves of freezing water washed over the deck of the Saint Desmond as she struggled from the crest of one wave to the trough of the next. Four days out of Shanghai the gale had blown up from over open water and now, 36 hours into the storm, her crew was weary and spent, but still the winds blew.

Inside the vessel, mournful wails of over stressed rivets and metal took turns with the peals of thunder in a macabre concerto, she had been built to withstand such torture 18 years ago, but 18 years is a long time to a ship like the Saint Desmond. Captain Tumaine rubbed his temples as he tried to chase a cup of lukewarm coffee. Charts lay before him and a decent amount of electrical gadgetry beeped and blipped in the background, trying to reassure him that everything would be OK. Right now, Claude Tumaine wasn't so sure.

It seemed a bit clichéd, this was to be his last voyage commanding a cargo ship across the open seas, a desk job beckoned in San Francisco and his wife of only two years had made it quite plain that his love affair with the waves could be fed just as easily on weekends with a beer in his hand as it could five days out of Shanghai in a warhorse fighting long odds. He sighed, knowing better than to curse the fate that befell him, the sea is a fickle mistress and better men than he had died trying to tame her. He stood and looked out through the window.

Rain spit down on his vessel, the drops were vanquished by wipers and replaced just as quickly with others bearing even more moisture. Maybe it was just as well, the ocean was not something he wanted to see right now. Rolling waves 18 feet high tossed the ship about and the water seethed beneath them. When a wave contradicted their course, its watery fingers doused everything on the deck and tried to find entrance in the hold below. More often than not now, the waves succeed. The bilge pumps almost never stopped pumping.

Captain Tumaine saw the light at almost the same time the mate called out "Land Ahead!" He scrambled to find their positions on the map, there it was, a small lighthouse on a rocky rise 100 miles from their destination. "Hard to Port!" He shouted out, knowing that they had plenty of foes and few allies at this point. The rolling waves tried to push them onto the rocks, the ferocious wind did the same, only inertia and her twin screws could save the ship now. Tumaine held his breath.

Through the body of the ship could be heard a scraping, the likes of which he had heard once before and desperately had not wanted to repeat. It lasted for a second or two, and then they were around the rocks. Captain Tumaine let out his breath and listened to the damage report "nothing visible down here Captain" with a sigh of relief. Maybe, just maybe, this trip wasn't meant to be a cliché after all. He looked forward to recounting his last voyage with a beer in his hand some Saturday soon.

The End

Liquids and Solids are nice, but I'm a Vapor man

His mouth tasted like the inside of a sweaty baseball mitt, he smacked his lips together twice before realizing he didn't want to do it again. His head throbbed with the after effects of too much domestic beer followed by too little sleep. He heard the sound again, it was louder this time, louder and closer, and he wanted it to stop.

After the third try, his eyelids opened, slightly crusty from congealed goo that had deposited in the night. The light that filtered through was harsh and brassy, not the soft light of midmorning through lightly rustling curtains, but the inquisitive light that demands to know where you were last night and what exactly you thought you were doing. On second thought, it wasn't the light; it was his girlfriend Carrie who wanted to know these things. Either way, in depth analysis had somehow skipped his to-do list this morning, replaced by sleep, rehydrate, and regurgitate, most likely in that order.

The noise went on, like angry bees trying to get into his skull through his ears, he opened his eyes again and noticed that it was coming from his girlfriend. Hadn't she given up yet? Apparently not. He noticed that she had large breasts which got him thinking that maybe he should make some attempts to be civil. "Mmammph" he managed to get out before she started in again.

Memories began to eke their way insidiously into his conscious mind, tearing noisily through the amnesia of state dependent memory. He remembered a girl who wasn't his girlfriend, and two guys who were friends that seemed to want him to go home with this other girl. He recalled stolen kisses in the back of a car (it may well have been his) and a slap at some other point. He couldn't really say it if was before or after. The scent of perfume had been lying innocuously in his nostrils until this point but it decided to make itself known as a bit of punctuation behind the memory. Inwardly he groaned. Outwardly too.

Up on one arm now, he confronted the wraith who continued to verbally assault him. It appeared that combinations of words such as "Um... nothing" and "I guess I could have" seemed not to be helping his position. He closed his mouth for a moment and willed wise words to come to him. The wise words were still asleep it seemed and she began again.

"I can't believe you would do that to me, don't you know how humiliating it's going to be? I have to face those people again Mark, what am I going to say? They know you left with a woman last night, and they know that I know..." the dialogue seemed to be destined to continue in this manner for quite some time. It was time, time to employ the secret weapon. Summoning the powers of concentration and cheap beer, he focused, gurgled, and let loose with a powerful fart, one with both duration and substance. "Jesus, you're so immature. We'll talk about this later" and then she was gone.

Settling into the embrace of the slightly sweat soaked sheets, Mark approached Nirvana once more, sneaking in through the back door.

The End

Captain of the Deep

Visionary prophecy from the mind of Dan Marvin

The rusty hull of the old freighter shone in the lights of the diver's sled. He first saw the gaping hole, showing where the ship had met with its untimely demise. Around the wreck was the debris of a commercial vehicle, various cans that had held solvents, some unidentifiable bits of metal, trash. Not a very impressive assortment to signify that man had once conquered the seas in this vessel!

Inside the hull, the temperature was cooler; he could feel it through his suit. The sun never shone here and the inhabitants were a bit annoyed with his intrusive light. Undaunted by the doleful glares of the fish, he swam forward, the first cognizant creature to ply the halls of the ship in 40 years or more.

The galley came first, a twisted maze of metal, tables, and carnage. A few of the crew had been caught dining, it seemed. Of all the things a man could be doing when he died, eating seemed the most human. The bulkhead was agape, showing the living quarters down the hall. He ventured into one and was immediately sorry he had done so. 40 years and many fish had not been kind to the sailor still trapped in his loft.

The engine room brought up the rear, messy machinery that still appeared to be trying to power the stricken vessel, caught in mid stroke and dying every bit as gracefully as the Captain must have 5 decks above. The water had apparently entered here first; no one was left to tend the machinery, even in death.

On the way up, he stopped at the recreation facilities; there was still a void near the top of the room. Apparently, he had not been the only one to find it although he would be the only one to leave it. He looked at the ping pong tables and a scattered deck of watery cards. His fins stirred some of them up, 3 aces disintegrated before his mask.

On the bridge, the true story was told. The Captain was buckled into a seat in front of the radio. He had honorably served the vessel and her crew; he could not have known that the radio never sent his cries for help all those years ago. A few lost souls kept him company, dutiful officers to the end.

As he neared the surface, the diver turned for one last look at the empty hull. There was no treasure here, at least nothing he could spend. Her final words were not as grand as those of the Titanic, not as mystical as a pirate ship; the only footnote the freighter would write in the history books was a warning. "The sea is no place for the faint of heart."

The End

Marv and the Orchids

Two molecules were flitting around one day when they felt on overwhelming attraction for each other. He had a couple of electrons just sitting out there doing nothing and she had an empty s orbital but they were so bulky they really didn't know how to get together. They spun around each other giving each other the (single atomic) eye but, alas, neither of them knew the right things to say or what to talk about. "What's your vibrational energy, baby?" he ventured boldly but she would just give off some red light (her equivalent of a blush) and say nothing.

One day, his friend stopped by to see how things were in the flask. He hadn't been around in awhile so he had a lot of catching up to do. "I'm a catalyst" the friend said. "I can get you two together if anyone can." The molecule was doubtful but it was worth a shot. The two floated over towards where she was spinning playfully and the catalyst went to work.

The catalyst knew all the right moves and soon he had her all lined up. When everything was ready, the catalyst motioned to his friend who came over sullenly. He had watched the moves the catalyst had put on his little organic molecule and he was steamed. "Come on over, there's someone I'd like you to meet!" The catalyst motioned for him to come closer. The attraction they had felt was even stronger now and they hit it off right away. When they started to covalently bond, the catalyst moved off to join two more frustrated molecules. What a great job he had!

The End

The Lackey

Uncommon insight for the common man by Dan Marvin

The light mist of a midday shower flew in his face as he raced his bicycle homeward but Leon was much too busy to notice. The bag of groceries in the basket teetered precariously but the canned goods strategically located kept it rooted. As he rounded the last corner, an orange flew out. There was no time to get it, it rolled into the road and was summarily crushed under the tire of a passing motorcar.

He leapt from the bicycle, grabbed the bag, and raced into the house. The silence told him that she was not home yet and he was just as glad. He needed a few minutes to get dinner started and pick up, the house was a mess. As the food began to simmer, he heard the car door slam and he cowered a bit inwardly, awaiting the onslaught.

His wife blew into the house like a storm cloud, strewing clothes and issuing demands. "Is dinner ready? Why aren't my shirts facing the same way? What is this spot on my socks?" As she changed, Leon picked up the discarded clothing and checked on dinner.

With a magic touch he produced a dinner fit for kings, or at least his Queen, garnishing the plate just so with a sprig of parsley, arranging it so no item touched the one next to it, and making sure that everything was hot without being too hot. Knowing that none of the extra attention would be appreciated or even noticed, he brought the meal into the dining room and laid it out on the table.

After a silent dinner of watching his wife eat, Leon retired to the living room for an evening of watching her favorite shows. He really didn't mind, he had long ago given up having an opinion about entertainment. With a watchful eye, he kept her glass filled with wine and brought out various snack foods as required. The hour grew late; he went in and turned down the bed.

As he finished his evening chores, he heard a strident "Leon, get in here! And bring the whipped cream!" from the bedroom. He smiled broadly. Who says being a lackey wasn't a good career choice?

The End

Dubious Definition – Broad jump (n) the motion made by a broad when startled.

Unaffiliated and Unafraid

An inflammatory call to arms by Dan Marvin

When he opened his eyes, there was a peaceful moment of ignorant bliss to greet Samuel DeTom. The blurry objects around him could be palm trees, a hammock, and bikini clad women. The thin smile that touched his lips was soon banished by the flood of conscious that came unbidden from the light.

With a start, he sat bolt upright and began to throw on clothes. The floor held a fine assortment; he quickly had his day's wardrobe picked out. A baseball cap finished the ensemble and he grabbed a nutritious Pop Tart breakfast on the way out the door. He leapt onto his bike and began to pedal like mad. Having his license revoked was a bit of a blessing, really.

His lungs gave forth some of the smoke he had forced them to inhale the night before in the form of gooey green material. It being biodegradable, he reasoned, the ground would make a fine place to begin the delicate dance of microbes that would turn the material into nutrient rich loam. His expectoration was robust.

Sam turned the corner to his building at last and threw the bike into the concealing weeds beside it. Two at a time, he ran up the stairs, said "Hi" to Delores, and was at his cubicle by 8:01. Not bad. The CRT flickered brightly and sprang to life, ready to begin the steady progression of information that some people had, others wanted, and he delivered.

At noon, the vending machine disgorged a fine ham sandwich for his enjoyment. He ate the tasteless morsel in two seconds and chased it down with a Diet Coke. Sated, he made small talk with the dork across the hall and watched the secretaries walk through the maze of cubicles. The afternoon held no surprises and he was glad when the day was through.

About 6PM, Sam began to awake. Sitting on his couch with a sub and a smoke, he watched extreme skiing for awhile and decided to go out. His roommate had already gone to work and they didn't hang out much anyway. Always one girl or other causing problems between them. He threw on a jacket and some Obsession for Men and headed out the door.

A round of beer became five, a bummed smoke became six, and the same friends surrounded him as had the night before. Although the stories were different, they felt the same. Late, he grabbed a cab and hit his bed at 3AM. 4 and a half hours later the alarm sounded. Only three more days until the weekend.

The End

- Marvin is a powerful voice for his generation. My only problem is that he isn't saying much with it. -Seattle Post Dispatch Tribuner Daily

The Scientific Method

Methodical fiction by Dan Marvin

An eat signal went through the biomass that passes for a Denaurian brain. With the greatest finesse, the creature picked up 300 tons of Denaurian soil and swallowed it. As opposed to a muscular contraction, swallowing for the Denaurian was a series of air blasts that sent the soil through a system of screens.

Screen number one pulled out the oversized indigestibles, largish rocks, trunks of trees, vacation homes. The remaining entrained matter was divided by a series of air lances into digestible and indigestible items in the gullet of the creature. Tom was most disheartened to find himself consigned to the "digestible" tract.

As he made his way into the center of the beast, his journey facilitated by the remaining 150 tons of food, he had plenty of time to examine a Denaurian first hand. Their knowledge of the natives was so slight. Since several years could go by until one was hungry, the contact had been brief, sporadic, and generally fatal. He turned on the recorder periodically and made notations.

He began by analyzing the area in which he found himself. A staging area of sorts, he wondered what passed for enzymes in a creature this large. Very shortly thereafter, he became quite sorry he had wondered. A parasitic arrangement found a 3 ton beetle doing shuttle duty. It picked up pieces of this and that and sent them into the digestive tract. Very soon, it had sensed Tom's presence.

He had only screamed a bit and run circles until he tripped over a pile of digestive beetle excrement. When next he came to, he decided his professional curiosity might have been better suited by studying the Denaurian from afar. Too late for regrets, he continued his way into the stomach.

Ahead, there was a loud noise coming from around the bend. He told himself not to wonder what it was, the memory of the digestive beetle still firmly in mind. He and the turf on which he was riding made the bend and he saw the large stones which aided the digestive process.

A probe located and recovered the recorder from Tom's belt; belt still attached, and dutifully began its trip back to the lab. Tom's painful ride through the digestive tract would be cataloged and reviewed by the next available scientist. Unfortunately, cutbacks by the science Ministry meant that his sacrifice wouldn't be noted for another 730 years by which time the Denaurians were extinct.

The End

Chapter 1 - Deceit!

The inner voices of her soul gave Captain Rhiannon pause as the yawning divide of space spread out before them. The immense void of blackness sprinkled decoratively with stars always gave her a thrill when seen stripped of a masking atmosphere. This time was especially poignant; she was on the command deck of her first ship, her first command, the *Hawthorne*.

Captain Rhiannon briefly scanned the mission sheet, as if she hadn't memorized it by now, and gave the order. "Console, please set in a target of track 243B01, the Negune cluster. Deviate 3 degrees at track 87G015 to account for stellar shift."

"The target is set." The word came up from Con 1. He had also memorized the mission; the target had been set since 07:56:13, twelve seconds after getting the green light. After years of laboring in the bowels of spaceliners like the *Hawthorne*, he was finally getting his chance on deck. At the "go" signal, the Hawthorne eased slowly out of airdock and began to accelerate. She was on her way.

Captain Rhiannon listened to the unfamiliar hum of the thrust generators and sensed more than felt the dampened acceleration. Around Decalight 3, she got the usual nausea but it quickly passed. It was a routine mapping mission of a track already well mapped. She was not sure if the general had been being patronizing by giving her an easy assignment or if there was more to it. She decided to go bottomside and meet more of her crew.

Meanwhile, in the depths of the *Hawthorne*, no one heard the ominous 'ping' emanating from a smallish, undistinguished box laying on the energy feed of TG #1. Although small of stature, if undetected it proved to play a large part in the maiden command of Captain Rhiannon.

The End

Phractured Philosophy – Considering almost all of us start out as a head, two arms, two legs, and a body, there sure are a lot of variations on that theme.

The Testament of Patience

Fictitious fiction from Dan Marvin

A cold breeze awoke "Seven Cities of War" from its slumber. A window must be open. In a way he was put out, who were these people to interrupt his slumber with a freezing chill? In another way, he was a book, not at all likely to have a reason to wake up on his own.

With a cellulose yawn, he looked around. Sure enough, Marvin the window stood wide open, he could see the sunshine in the yard outside. A bit of stirring at the curtain told him the day was sunny but windy. He breathed in the fresh air gratefully, the discomfiture of being disturbed giving way to the pleasure of a clean spring day and the fresh air replacing stale.

Eight years ago he had been formed; the agony of birth was still in his mind. A large binding machine had bore him and he had been pushed into the cruel world never to see his mother again. Into a crate, and rushed by truck to a distribution center with his clones. In a way, it had been an idyllic life, stuck in a carton on a shelf somewhere, free from worry and surrounded by others just like him. Still, he was happy when the freedom forklift had arrived and rescued them.

His trip into the living room was a blur. He vaguely remembered store shelves, a book signing, and the trip home in a brown paper sack. Finally, his purpose had become clear. He divulged his information to the eyes of three readers, two adults and a teen. The teen had treated him poorly; his spine still ached from the toil of educating the whole crew. Still, it had been fitting and right, he had fulfilled his destiny.

A new face peered up at him. What was this? Another reader? "Seven Cities of War" grew excited! Here was a chance to be useful once more! The hand attached to the face selected several others. He began to feel a sense of dread. What if he was not deemed worthy? What if the face was looking for comedy or romance? What if it only wanted a crossword puzzle? A bit of dew broke out on his cover.

Ah, the hand had selected him. With joy, he rode into the other room. At last, some other person to read him! The feeling of pride swelled up inside him. It did not, however, last for long. Stacked on top of the dictionary and the Bible, "Seven Cities of War" felt the buttocks of a small child being placed upon him. Resolutely, he bore the shame of being a booster seat.

The End

Common maladies of the outer ear

Irrational ponderings by Dan Marvin

Guidance cut out, they were adrift in space. The *Hawthorne* floated forlornly just outside an asteroid belt in the Fastule Prime Star Cluster, an unfriendly place given to fits of highly charged radiation bursts. If they could not get the engines back on-line, they were doomed; it was as simple as that.

Captain Rhiannon paced restlessly around the bridge. The peculiar debilitation was not covered in the Ops Manuals and she was afraid she might miss something. A fact finding mission to a well mapped track was not supposed to be a test of mettle but a routine 6 month stay on route to a real command. This was her first ship; she did not want it to be her last.

Convinced that there was nothing more to do on the bridge, she headed to the thrust center. Scurrying engineers swarmed around her, barely acknowledging her presence, much less saluting. She was mildly annoyed but put it behind her, the pressure was getting to everyone. "What is the status, vigil?" She asked the ranking officer.

"Engines 1 and 3 are off line for diagnosis. Engine 2 is showing 100% output but the thrust is negligible. We've had all three firing wide open, we should have been in decalight range by now. I'm not sure what is happening." Chief vigil Warren's voice was showing the effects of the pressure.

"Captain, solar flare beginning to erupt on Fastule B. Not a big one, but significant."

"How are our shields, vigil?" She asked, knowing full well the answer. In fact, she got none, just a sidelong glance that said it all. "What if, instead of fighting the solar winds, we ride them out?" she asked, suddenly struck with inspiration. "Let's turn sideways and cast a large parachute of tribinium fibers to catch the energy burst." It seemed plausible.

Grunting in a manner that implied he was less than thrilled with the directive, Chief vigil Warren began giving the orders. The deed was done, if it worked they were saved, if not they were fried.

On the bridge, Captain Rhiannon paced even more furiously. "Any motion, helm?" She asked. "None Captain" the reply. "Wait, yes, we're starting to move! Sound 1... Sound 2... We're clear of the asteroid belt... stabilizing at Sound 2.7... We're moving!" The cheer went up about the cabin.

5 minutes later, the energy draining field surrounding asteroid 13047-B lessened as it was filled with solar particles. The engines on the *Hawthorne* started to thrust and the shields returned. A collective sigh of relief rang throughout the vessel. Captain Rhiannon relaxed inwardly and ordered Chief vigil Warren beheaded.

The End

The Framingham Farce

A play in 3 acts by Dan Marvin

Over the ashen white plains of February rode the warriors of Eidelham, the scent of victory intoxicating their brains. Yon lie the high country of which the oracle had spake, his directions had proved true. They saw the outcropping that looked liked the head of an ass, swerved right and rode up the divide of unrest. The setting sun pointed their way, they saw the yawning mouth of the cave.

Far behind on his pack mule, Roderic brought up the rear. Laden with the provisions of a crusade, his was the job of the common man. He carried, cooked, cleaned, and bore the brunt of countless crude jokes. Still, deep down he knew that he would make a fearless knight.

The cryptic runes on the cave wall pointed straight up. They looked above and shouted, "Roderic, bring the ladder! And be quick about you!" With ladder in foot, they climbed, into the ceiling room. Like stalagmites, the frozen forms of tens of men stood in mute testimony to the magic of the place.

Roderic waited until the last lord had ascended and then waited a bit more. He began to climb. As he had suspected, a foot found the top of his head and pushed him down. Undaunted, he began to climb once more. He had to see the mystery of the changing rock.

The frozen remains of past travelers were pushed aside. All the men in the room looked about them; none wanted to be the first to peer into the pit of his own soul. Still, the pool lay beckoning, great power to he who was pure of spirit, a frozen eternity to he with sin. One by one, they walked forth and looked. One by one, they screamed and became one with the rock...

Roderic watched in horror as the brigade dwindled away. He could not believe that one of these gallant fellows wasn't the saint the prophecy foretold. Sir Isaan walked forward, looked at Roderic, and peered into the pool. He was the last of the party to get stiff.

Roderic looked about him. "My Lord!" he bellowed "what horror hath thou wrought?" A voice boomed at him, "Look ye into the pool, Sir Roderic! He who is of simple means is of pure heart!" Roderic hastened forward and peered into the abyss. As his extremities began to petrify, he cursed the Lord under his breath. God got quite a chuckle out of it.

The End

A Bandwagon for Bob

Thinky fiction by Dan Marvin

A shuttle bus passed by and the old bag lady huddled closer to her fire. It was cold here. Probably the temperature more than anything else. The bag lady, Imelda, was not feeling the cold or seeing the shuttle bus. Inside her head all was warm and thoughts came freely without undue influence from the outside. Imelda was at peace.

A van pulled up beside her and a well meaning young man stepped from the passenger door. Pulling his coat tighter, he walked to Imelda and shook her gently. Her eyes opened and she peered at the freshly shaven face of the man standing over her. His eyes were caring (like HIS eyes, Imelda thought) but with an intense blue that made one take notice. The face ruggedly handsome (the thought of another face like this in another time came to Imelda) with a square chin and strong features.

"Imelda?" said the face. "Are you Imelda?"

"Wrong person!" she said it more harshly than she had intended.

"Sorry to disturb you ma'am." The face intoned.

As the young man walked back to the van, Imelda contented herself by the fire once more. So much like HIM, she thought. Hadn't they once had a son, in that far off life?

He got in the van and said to the driver, "nope, she said she wasn't Imelda.

Strange, she looked so much like the pictures. Maybe the next one." And off they drove.

The End

Questionable Quotation – "What God hath joined together, let no man rend asunder. Even if you knew how to rend something asunder, which most likely you don't."

- Book of Uncommon Prayer

The Hogfat Ado

Fatty fiction by Dan Marvin

It was a dark Thursday. The sort of dark Thursday where there isn't much light. You know the type. Clouds hung over the sky. Maybe that's why it was so dark, who knows? I was working the early morning shift. That's the shift where you work when it's early morning. Maybe that's why they call it that. Before I knew it, She came into my life. She was wearing a cheap fur stole, the kind which doesn't cost much because it's cheap. Still, I could see she was all lady. A real dame.

She waltzed into the room like she owned the place. I never had met the owner so maybe she did. I guess you could say I didn't know and you'd be right 'cuz I didn't. She sat on the desk and produced a card. The kind of card which is most effective when you read it because then you can glean the information it contains. That kind of card.

The card said simply "Hogfat" (editor's note: These stories rarely pertain to the title so take note, this is an historic moment). I stared at the card and read it again. Sure enough, I hadn't been mistaken; it still said "Hogfat."

"What's this mean?" I asked. I asked that because I didn't know. Honestly.

She said "You think I'm a cheap fluzy maybe?" I said I hadn't and it was true because I thought she was just a dame in a cheap fur stole. That's all. She flounced out of the office as quick as she had flounced in. I was confused but quickly forgot it. These things happened on the early morning shift. I heard a crack and looked up. The ceiling was falling in. You know, when the ceiling was up there before but suddenly it's...

The End

Fabricated Factoid –

78 – Percentage of travelers in recent poll that thought customer service of major airlines had declined in the last five years.
100 – Percentage of major airlines who would never admit it but think deep down that passengers should just stop whining already.

Begging Your Pardon

Contemporary fiction by Dan Marvin

Huddled in the cave, the Nebunancer family waged their final battle against overwhelming odds. Three weeks earlier the mutants had driven them from their home (itself built like a fortress) and forced them to seek shelter in the secluded cave which they had saved for an emergency. Now the mutants had found them (tracked by their smell, no doubt) and were breaking through the door. In a final fit of energy, Mr. Nebunancer hurled the energy saucer at the sagging door. With a burst of unreal, dazzling light, the saucer exploded sending the mutants in all directions. The Nebunancer family was safe, but for how long?

Meanwhile, light years across the galaxy, Bob and June were sitting down for a quiet family meal with Espentio, their first and only child. Espentio hated his name and had developed quite a neurosis from it. He arrived at the dinner table wearing his finest gas diversion equipment so as to be safe from any tear gas canisters lobbed through the window. Sure enough, just as he sat down, in came the tear gas. As his parents were writhing in agony, unable to see, Espentio calmly picked up the canister and threw it back onto the street below. Only then did he realize that he was in full view of the snipers on the roof opposite. He ducked, but not in time, as the bullet glanced from the window sill and tore into is chest cavity.

In the next county, trails of ice crystals crisscrossed the otherwise cloudless sky leaving evidence of the passing airplanes for all to see. On the ground, paths crisscrossed the field of clover and grass leaving evidence of the passing animals for all to see. Unfortunately for Leon, no evidence was apparent of the flu germ that made its way from his hand into his nose. In a few days, there would be plenty of evidence.

Next to the bubbling brook, a beautiful maiden sat in the embrace of a handsome prince. They were only statues though, so nothing exciting happened until acid rain and wind had worn them down to two formless lumps of rock.

The End

Fabricated Factoid –
1010% - increase in pharmaceutical advertising in the last 20 years
1010% - increase in diagnosed maladies in the last 19 years, 11 months.

Bart and the Bard

Contemporary B fiction by Dan Marvin

In the farthest land of the Seven Mountains, lived a Boneydue, one of the seven sons of Boffydee. In his cave, he lived a quiet existence far from the pressures exerted by outside influences. His wants were simple, food for the table, rest after a hard days work, and a large sport coupe with ample engine space to blow away the punks who lived nearby. The car was kept at a constant temperature of 32 degrees C, thereby to protect it from the ravages of temperature fluctuation. Boneydue (actually, Boneydue II fourth cousin of Boneydue the Younger) kept the coupe in a sealed garage bringing it out only on special occasions.

One day, Boneydue heard a knock on the cave door. Such a simple thing, a knock, yet this one brought fear to his heart and he barely could get up the courage to look to see who it could be. Standing there was a man in a hard hat that looked every bit the construction worker. He noticed Boneydue's eye peeping through the hole and he flourished a paper where Boneydue could see it.

"You're gonna have to move, Boneydue II, a superhighway is coming through!" The construction worker said this in a way resembling simple poetry, as if he had indeed said it before.

"This is my home!" Boneydue replied. He looked around him at a lifetime of collection treasures, his simple but comfortable furniture, and his table already set for dinner. And of course his customized hot rod sitting at 32 degrees in the garage.

"And this is a writ of extradition," said the worker, pushing the paper under the door and walking off. Boneydue II heard the sound of roaring machinery, getting ever closer. He ran to the garage and started the car. This would be close! With a state approaching panic, he opened the door with the automatic garage door opener. Would it never open? His mind raced. At last, the door was open enough to squeeze through.

Suddenly, government funding for the highway was cut off and it was decided that Boneydue could remain in his cave. That night, Boneydue got very drunk.

The End

Aboriginal Sin

Early fiction from Dan Marvin

Earl got out of bed and jumped into the shower, vitally impaling himself on a spear that a careless aborigine had left upright in the shower stall. "Whoops," Earl reasoned, "Guess I should always look before jumping into the shower." In a fit of rage, he told the aborigine whom he had been housing to get his stuff out of the house by the next day. The aborigine pulled his spear from Earl's abdomen, gathered his loin cloth and left. Earl then slumped to the floor lifeless.

Once outside, the aborigine felt much better. He had hated being cooped up in that house with Earl and now felt much more at home (even though Elm Street did not look appreciably similar to the outback of Australia). He changed his name to Altimor and ambulated swiftly westward.

When he reached California, he placed his ear on the ground and gave a listen. What he heard there made him put forth the following hypothesis: "ugh, garumbo dodobean." This meant, in Altimor's language (a private dialect known only to himself, one reason he had been forced to leave Australia) "California is about to undergo a massive geological upheaval, falling irresistibly into the sea." Sure enough, Montana slipped slowly into the core of the earth.

Seeing this unlikely occurrence, Altimor went on a series of talk shows telling how he had predicted the destruction of California and then seen Montana slip slowly into the core of the earth. Everyone was fascinated not by what Altimor said (no one could understand him anyway) but by the huge growth on the side of his neck which looked surprisingly like a full grown bullfrog.

The End

The Asparagus of Lincoln Road

Fiction for a vegetative state by Dan Marvin

The cabbages lay in the heat, unable to get out of the sun, whether by their lack of motivation (i.e. feet) or just laziness, no one knew. It was apparent, though, that they would shrivel or die unless some rain came soon. It looked desperate for farmer Bob.

"Them damn cabbages won't go into the shade" he expostulated. It had been a rough month. None of the farmers could coax their produce to seek out the shelter of the nearby woods. All they could hope for was a rain, and quick, or else this would be another year without income. Farmer Bob wondered why they had ever evolved from gatherers.

At least this gave him some extra time to think about the existential pleasures of being a farmer. Often he would sit and meditate, wondering about his role in the universe and why the damn cabbages were so lazy. It finally dawned on him the cabbages probably had not realized that they could escape the sun unless they knew that shade was cooler. With that, he jumped up and ran out to the fields.

As they saw him coming, the cabbages leapt up and ran away, afraid for their lives. Farmer Bob watched them go and suddenly realized that all he had had to do was throw a little fear into them. Wild with joy, he ran unwittingly into the road and was struck by a heard of marauding lima beans.

That is the reason that no one likes lima beans to this day.

The End

Erroneous Excerpt – "'Nevermore' quoth the Raven, after eating a greasy hamburger, fries, and a chocolate shake all in one sitting."

Edgar Allen Po'boy

Innocuous Fluff

Fiction with just a hint of Chardonnay by Dan Marvin

A deep, steaming cleft rent the earth and from it flowed the blood of nations long dead. The sea boiled away and what was left turned to blood, killing the fish and all the creatures of the sea. The sky turned red and hideous sounds of wailing and gnashing of teeth made the earth tremble. The trees caught fire and all the forests of the earth were burned to a smoking ruin. The sun turned into a scorching ember, burning the flesh and leaving no refuge on the face of the earth. The animals died, the crops withered, life ceased to exist. A trail of souls floated peacefully above the din, those who had lived a righteous life, and many more were beaten on the road to Hell, there to live in eternal damnation.

Meanwhile, on the dark side of the earth, Bernie and Amanda turned on their air conditioners to ward off the inexplicable heat and turned the stereo on quietly to block out the wailing and teeth gnashing going on outside their abode. Amanda commented that it sounded as if there was a great gnashing of teeth going on but Bernie said it was probably just the wind. Without paying heed to the burning of the forests outside, they settled in for a night of watching TV. Amanda turned on the TV and saw only static. With icy certainty, they realized that the end of the earth was certainly upon them...

The End

Questionable Quotation – "The only thing we have to fear, is fear itself. Except for zombies of course, the living dead creep me out big time." - FDR

Irritatingly Cute Story

A story in which life imitates art by Dan Marvin

It was another day in Snurfle village. The type of day where the sun shines giving you daylight hours and then the sun goes away giving you night. You know the type. I was working the day shift. That's the shift where it's day out when you work and that's why they call it the day shift. I was walking the beat out by the Toadstool projects. That's when you make a house in a toadstool like Smurfs only different 'cuz you're not. They were the new projects where the poor Snurfles lived. You know the type, they're poor 'cuz they don't have any money. That's what I always figured.

At four o'clock I got the call. It was the type of call that makes you worried because it comes right on the walky-talky and you answer it. You know the type. It seemed the colorful furry Snurfles down by the Toadstools were having an insurrection again. I was worried because I wasn't unworried. Mainly that. The colorful furry Snurfles that live in the Toadstools are real SOB's, low class customers. There was Lazy Snurfle, Hungry Snurfle, Cutthroat Snurfle, Foodstamp Snurfle, and Mangler The Killer Snurfle. They were all drunk and rowdy. I checked my gun. It was there. That was a big help because you want your gun to be there when you think you might need it. It's just one of those things.

I went down to Fourth and Toadstool where the riot was in progress. That's when it's going because someone started it and no one bothered to stop. You know the type. Anyway, it looked like someone had started a picnic and were singing cute little songs. You know, the type of cute little song where you're really irritated because no one in real life sings 'em. They offered me a piece of chicken. The type of chicken that can't really exist because Snurfles are so small there can't be chicken that size. It's always been a problem. I bit into it and started to choke. The kind of choking where you get a bone in your throat and only have a few seconds to get it out or it's...

The End

Dubious Defnition – Flighty (adj) the opposite of swimmy

Welcome to the Wasteland

Fiction for those with great intestinal fortitude by Dan Marvin

I stood looking into the undergrowth as the growls continued to emanate from therein. I wondered as to the source but, wisely, kept my mouth shut as there was no one at which to inquire anyway. It seems that I had been in the jungle for months as my clothes were tattered and my beard was shaggy but I really had no recollection of any of the events leading up to my being here. It was an enigma but all things are it seems. I recalled wondering if someone were to contract amnesia if they would not remember proper grammatical structure and any vocabulary they might have accrued in their years before. It seemed unlikely since I not only remembered "amnesia" I also remembered "grammatical" and "accrued" as well as having had the thought. There were many answers to questions I had previously had. But then, was it true amnesia if I could remember questions I had had about amnesia? It was clarifying but confusing. I pondered as I wandered...

A wandering band of aborigines caught me and tied me hand and foot. It seemed a bit odd but since I had amnesia, I figured it might just have been the way of the land. How was I to know? I went peacefully. As they spirited me away, I realized that a roving band of aborigines seemed somewhat out of place in the jungle. The thought quickly vanished as I realized that I might have been stupid in real life so I wouldn't have had to worry about such things. The thought was comforting.

As we approached their village, they bound me quite snugly to a tree and performed a ritual not entirely dissimilar to drawing straws. Then, one of the braves (apparently the loser) came to my tree and drew his knife. He slashed my bonds and handed me another knife (primitive thing, I thought) indicating I should fight him. While it was unlikely that I was a good knife fighter in my previous life, the chance was there so I accepted. We sparred briefly and suddenly I remembered everything! I was the sole keeper of a plan for world peace which simply had to be brought before the council of world elders. As I pondered this, the soap opera on which I was a character was summarily canceled and I faded slowly out of existence...

The End

Froggy's Evolution

Dinner was a joyous affair in Costone Mansion and after the food was eaten and the last compliment was given, the guests contentedly retired to the sitting room for a snifter of brandy before they retired to their individual homes. Mrs. Costone was far and away the best hostess on the island and all of the guests loved it when she threw one of her parties.

On the other side of the island, old Mrs. Hobbson sat alone again listening to the faint sounds of merriment coming from Costone Mansion. She looked at the can of beans simmering on the fire and wondered if she would ever be invited to one of the gala events. As she was sitting at the window, engrossed in her daydream, there came a timid tapping on the door. Mrs. Hobbson hobbled to the door and slowly lifted the latch. The visitor was little Timmy from down the lane.

"Mrs. Hobbson," started Timmy, "what were you thinking about? I could see you through the window."

"Oh, nothing Timmy. Just a silly dream of mine. I was thinking how nice it would be to be invited to the Costone's for dinner just once."

"Why don't you ask them?" Timmy queried

"They wouldn't want an old crow like me at one of their parties," she somberly responded.

Long after he had left Mrs. Hobbson's, Timmy was thinking about what he could do to get her invited. As he lay in bed, a plan developed. He would visit Mrs. Costone the next day.

It was bright and sunny as Timmy started out to the mansion. He knocked on the door and was shown into Mrs. Costone's day room. He explained Mrs. Hobbson's dream as the hostess listened patiently and eventually elicited a promise for an invite to the next dinner. Sure enough, when the next dinner was to be given, an invite reached old Mrs. Hobbson. She wore the beautiful dress she had saved for all these years and everyone loved her. From there on out, every party at Costone Mansion had the traditional great food, good times, and Mrs. Hobbson.

(People have been saying I should have a story with a happy ending. Here it is and I hope you all enjoy it. If you don't, feel free to add the following supplemental ending:)

Mrs. Costone listening to Timmy babble on with an increasing amount of anger. How dare this little urchin traipse into her house and tell her who should be on her guest list? With a wave of her hand, she told the butler to dispose of little Timmy. As his body plummeted out of the door, he landed on top of a shocked Mrs. Hobbson. She scolded him for his stupid attempt and told him never to come to her cottage again. He developed deep psychological scars and had to be hospitalized in a mental institution until the age of 30 when he developed a phobia towards being outdoors and cowered in a cave on a remote part of the island.

If wishes were fishes

A finely fried mess by Dan Marvin

The thunder boomed like the clap of godly hands, the water washed down in unswerving torrents, filling the ditches which filled the creeks which filled the rivers which flowed as they had forever towards the sea. From inside his bedroom window, Tommy looked glumly at the gray sky. He held a baseball in his hand, dad had promised to play catch with him this afternoon. Now dad was downstairs "catching up on work" and mom was gone until 8 and his sister was busy reading which was something she loved and something he did when it was assigned as homework. With one last sigh, he turned from the gloomy picture outside and started to inventory the things in his room.

In the corner was his desk with the computer on it. He could turn on the computer, plug in one of the 73 assorted CD's and play a game for awhile. But he didn't really feel like it. He could turn on his gameboy, plug in one of the 73 assorted cartridges he had for it, but he didn't want to. He could put together the Harry Potter puzzle that his grandma had gotten him for his birthday, but he lacked the proper motivation. The legos that could be put together in a zillion different shapes would remain the epitome of chaos, at least for now. "I sure wish something exciting would happen" he opined.

Sighing again, Tommy looked back out the window, watching the streaks of rain as they dripped down the panes. He didn't hear the closet door open, didn't see the shape crawling into the room until... "Hello Tommy!" He nearly fell out of the window; he looked over just in time to see a clown greeting him, a fully dressed, fully made up, incredibly lifelike clown. "How ya doin'?" It asked him.

"Pretty good" stammered Tommy. He wasn't exactly shocked that a clown had appeared out of his closet, a steady diet of Nickelodeon cartoons hinted that such things could happen from time to time. What was more surprising was that the clown wasn't wet from the rain, his makeup appeared intact, and the handkerchief that emanated unendingly from his breast pocket was unscathed. Tommy watched in fascination as a wand turned into flowers, his toys became juggled, the clown performed backflips in the confines of his (messy) room, and similar clown feats were performed for him.

From his radio, circus music played. He swore he could smell peanuts and popcorn, heck he could almost hear the concessionaire walking towards him offering them up for sale. Rings magically clanged together, a firetruck appeared and the clown struggled valiantly with the hose. It wasn't too shocking when a tiger appeared from the closet, the clown did a hilarious 'tiger taming' act where he seemingly did everything wrong and yet the tiger obeyed. Tommy clapped and laughed.

After what seemed like ages, the clown approached Tommy, tussled his hair and looked down at him. "That'll be 485 bucks kid" the clown said.

"What?" asked an astounded Tommy.

"Look, wishes don't grow on trees; we're a profit making organization. You don't have the money?" Tommy shook his head emphatically. "Then I'm coming BACK kid, every week, on your allowance day. You're GOING to pay me 485 bucks or else!" And with that, the clown was gone, the only reminder of his presence the moldering pile of tiger dung on the carpet of Tommy's room.

The End

Fabricated Factoid –

8 – Percentage of ring tones on cell phones that are set to ring like a standard telephone
92 – Percentage of owners of those phones that get a smug satisfaction from rejecting the progress of ring tones, while overlooking the irony of not rejecting the progress of cell phones.

Arizona Justice

The hot tendrils of Arizona heat obscured the image of the rider on the next summit, parts of him looked close and parts were eerily missing. McKay's trained eye, however, knew the look of the man - trouble. He had been chasing strays all day and had happened on the tracks by accident. A few cows here, a few more there, the tracks leading off into the desert and a horse behind them, signs of rustling for sure.

He pulled the Winchester from its seat in the scabbard, and set his dapple in motion with the touch of his spurs. The horse started reluctantly, already tired from the midmorning sun and the hard miles chasing up and down steep arroyos. Still, his head came up and he put his heart into the slow trip to the next ravine.

When they got to where he had seen the outline of the rider profiled in the air, McKay looked at the hard packed ground. There was not much there to indicate that it had not been a mirage. Out of the corner of his eye, he saw a thin thread of smoke. Jerking his head around, he made out the still smoking butt of a cigarette, smoked not ten minutes before. He pulled his horse around and headed down the other side of the slope.

The hard earth turned to sand and the sand gave up only the occasional depression that might have been a horse track. Still, McKay knew that there must be a destination close by; driving cattle into the desert is a sure recipe for dead cattle. He was right. Several miles further and he started to see green, a small copse of trees surrounding a desolate water hole. He could smell the smoke from the branding fire.

Crouching and making his way towards the campsite, he was greeted to a typical western scene. Two men were holding down the cows and going over his "diamond d" brand turning it into a "pyramid 8" which very neatly covered it. A third, the man he had seen in the distance he thought, was roping the strays and bringing them to the fire. In two hours, they could have altered the brands on 50 cows; a whole day could net them 200. Not a bad day's work since they started with nothing.

McKay leveled the rifle at the two around the fire, stood, and walked in. His eyes took in the whole scene before the men noticed him. By the time they reached for their pistols, it was much too late, his Winchester belched smoke. The first man grabbed for his gut and plunged into the fire, the second grabbed his arm as it shattered. A quick shot at the man on the horse knocked him sprawling in the dirt and sent the horse running away, dragging the man for a ways before depositing him in the harsh Arizona sun.

The moans of the man with the shattered arm were heard for miles as McKay led him back to face the frontier justice of a desert cow town. If his conscience bothered him, he did not show it, his face was a mask of justice served.

The End

Birds of Paradise Lost

Avian fiction by Dan Marvin

With the grim determination of a bird possessed, One Caw collected himself and hurled himself at the barrier once more. He saw the sheen of the fire orb, reflected from the surface but he also saw "inside" a place more marvelous than he could imagine. There had to be a way in, there had to!

He had come from a poor family; theirs had been a timeworn nest on the wrong side of the field, away from the polite company of the tamer sparrows and doves. The blackbirds and crows had been his unruly playmates. Assuring himself he would never become like them, One Caw set out to find his center, his reason for being. He had built a snug nest with a female robin alongside the gutter on a suburban house, a nice little place if he did say so himself.

Every day, he threw himself into gathering, each grasshopper was a victory, and each beak he stuffed assured the continuation of his genes. For awhile, he lived the aviary dream. Then, it started to turn. His crow friends flew over frequently and taunted him. As they lay waste to the bird feeder out front, getting easy meals and living well, he continued to gather insects and worms. But the resentment grew.

One day, he ran into a blackbird he had known months ago, when he was young. The mischievous bird promised to show him a wonderful place, a place of infinite beauty and untold riches. He agreed. They sat on the deck of the human structure and looked "inside". Why was he not entitled to THIS, he thought. Why not him in front of the TV watching Wheel of Fortune? He began to devise a plan.

The other birds laughed at him as he began to tell them about "inside." Some, however, heard his evangelical words and began to share the vision with him. It was decided, he would lead them, he would show them the way to "inside." And so began his quest, the window would yield, it must!

After several hours of trying to get in the glass and failing each time, the human put up a screen. He clung to the screen for dear life until the human returned and forced him away. Again and again, he slammed into the sliding glass door, determined to lead his birds to the Promised Land. Again and again he was rebuffed.

Finally, another human was summoned. The BB penetrated One Caw's body and severed his spine. As he lay dying, he gathered together the other robins. "It is time," he said simply. "Let the offensive begin."

The End

Deadly Genes

Contemporary fiction by Dan Marvin

At the top of the trees, the weeping mist alit on branches already overburdened with ice and rolled down the bare branches, creating huge icicles. Throughout the forest, the audible "crack" of limbs giving up could be heard like minor explosions. Beneath the wintry disaster in the making, a human drama was unfolding. The footfalls were muffled by the icy pebbles as the small band made its way through the forest.

It was a family, wrapped in poorly insulated jackets, obviously taken by surprise by the early winter storm. The father, normally the leader, took up the rear to tend to any who would straggle. The mother walked up front, picking the way through years of underbrush, angling around already downed limbs and looking in vain for a light, a bit of color, anything that would tell them their long trek would at last bear fruit.

In the middle were a haggard set of twins and an older boy, all thoughts of protest gone, looking now just to survive against the huge odds facing the family. They plodded on with the vacant looks of ones long past their breaking points, reaching deep within themselves just to find the motivation to place one foot in front of the other for yet three more feet of travel.

The winter wind whipped at them, their constant companion for five days now. The packs on their backs were but clothes wrapped to carry their meager possessions. The thoughts of the broken down car, the lost path, the endless wandering were pushed out of their heads by the simple need to survive. It would be nightfall soon, time to think about finding shelter from the wind, trying to light a fire in an icestorm, and getting whatever sleep their weary bodies would allow them.

The mother stopped short and tested the air with her nose. Soon, the others smelled it too, the unmistakable smell of woodsmoke. They vainly looked around for the source for several minutes, casting this way and that, trying to detect from whence it came. At last, the trail was evident, and they came as close to running as their deadened feet would allow them.

The woodsmoke produced a cabin, the cabin heat, food, sleep, and a phone, the phone a taxi and a tow truck. After 6 days of wandering in the woods, they finally arrived at their destination and knocked on the door. It was answered by an oldish woman who welcomed them inside.

"Any trouble along the way?" Grandma asked. The family looked at each other and chuckled "No Granny," they lied "everything was fine." Grandma swore under her breath... she just had to think of another scheme to do them in...

The End

Beware Zombies Bearing Gifts

A warning shot heard round the world by Dan Marvin

The frost on the ground left the imprints of the feet running across it. In the midmorning sun, it would melt and leave the indelibly blackened footprints for many days to come. The feet were much less worried about the grass living then they were worried for their own life. Behind lay a scene of death, ahead the uncertain future of two men marked with an explosive secret.

Shale said to his brother as they ran "I can't believe I let you talk me into this, it's all your fault." The younger Morgan remained silent except for the explosive gasps of air he was taking to fill his demanding lungs. He would have shouted back that Shale knew what they were getting into, that he knew the risks, and that a million things could happen. Instead, he concentrated his attention on running and breathing.

At the bottom of the mountain, a badly mangled apparition arose from the rubble of the rockslide. Its head cocked to one side, not of curiosity but of several misplaced vertebrae. The oft-killed man began walking with a clumsy gait, easily following the tracks of the two running before him. Its face was a hideous mask of wreck and decay.

After a few minutes Shale and Slate Morgan stopped for a breather. "Do you think it's dead?" gasped Slate, still breathing heavy after several minutes. The question went unanswered or, rather, the answer was so obvious that it did not bear saying. How do you kill something that has been dead for 20 years? The day wore on and the Morgan's ran until they could run no more.

The sinking sun set the world ablaze just before it went away, a last reminder of life, it would seem. Shale and Slate settled in for a long, cold, uncomfortable night. As the night air crept around them, they began to sense that they were not alone.

In the morning, the sun rose again, as it always did. It glittered in the staring eyes of the two Morgan men, but they did not see it. Their now dead hands clutched Mary Kay cosmetics, enough for a complete makeover. The Mary Kay man had made his next sale.

The End

Questionable Quotation – When the world says "Give up", hope whispers "Try it one more time." When the world says "No thanks, we have enough", salesmen whisper "You can always use one more."

Wanted: Several lawyers to fight for this cause

Social commentary by Dan Marvin

The steam rolled off of the jungle floor in patches as the morning sun got to the business at hand, filtering through the trees to feed the teeming life below. Rufla the chimp sat enjoying one of the wayward rays. In the afternoon, when the fireball was at full intensity, he would seek out a dark place. For now, he let the heat sink into his bones and warm away the chill night air.

Kanku, one of the females, came over to him and displayed her genitalia. With a half hearted spurt of energy, they copulated. In a tender gesture, he grabbed the handful of fruit she had been eating and devoured it, leaving her hungry for more. The phrase "simians do it wild" flitted through his brain. Unfamiliar with English and not especially adept at double entendre, he ignored it.

He sauntered down to the water hole and drank as he eyed the carnivores warily. They seemed sated so he went back to the trees without becoming lunch. He dined on some leaf shoots and called to his friends with a raucous burst of hoots and wails. They responded, as monkeys do, and he found them nearby.

An unfamiliar scent caught his nostrils. It was acrid, like the smell of the lightning striking the earth. One of the elders screamed out "FIRE!" and the monkeys jumped around ineffectually. Disaster preparedness had never been one of their greater strengths. He stopped, dropped, and rolled but it did no particular good.

In the distance, the rumblings of earth movers and the calls of peasants could be heard echoing through the serene jungle setting. Rufla made his way past the zone of burning trees and looked at the smoldering debris on the other side. The peasants were tilling the still smoking soil. They would need leadership!

Rufla applied for a supervisor's job and started at $7.50 an hour. His squad despoiled the jungle faster than any other and was rewarded handsomely. He bought a used car and rented a modest apartment. He and Kanku were talking marriage until disaster struck. Full of indignation, environmentalists called for the end of clear cutting of the forest and Rufla was laid off. He turned to booze and died bitter, a not-so-subtle reminder of something we may have forgotten, millions of acres of jungle are clear cut yearly, providing good paying jobs for industrious jungle creatures.

The End

"You ripped it"

Protests from a two year old by Dan Marvin

In the nebulous gasses surrounding the Minula Prime star cluster, Org the energy cloud leisurely enjoyed the ripe protons the nearby sun was emitting. She sucked in a stream of them and watched distractedly as the sun from which they were coming went dark and cold.

She turned and eyed up a delicious looking red sun. Expanding her molecules in her own graceful way, she created a vacuum in the vacuum and caused the solar flares to come her way. The delicious plasma filled her with an immense sense of well being. After her hearty dinner, she slept for several eons.

The small luxury liner was sweeping majestically across the horizon, running full out as it made its way to the Galaxy Center Club Med. Her cargo of various sultans and political types enjoyed fine meals of wonderful food that she concocted out of unwanted cosmic matter and generally made merry.

The scanners on the luxury liner suddenly went full open, every one. They indicated huge concentrations of everything imaginable. The wise captain declared it to be a system wide malfunction and told the crew to continue on, unabated. Org looked at the small vessel coming her way and opened a small pseudopodia to accept it.

The craft nestled into the dock she had prepared and she went about draining its piddling energy resources. As the main engines drained, a small mixture of life energy from the sultans and politicians began to become entrained in the stream. The resulting heartburn made Org quite sick, and she belched the small space craft several million years into the future.

The End

Fabricated Factoid –

3 – Percentage of people in a recent test that stopped to help a man who had dropped a stack of papers in a NYC street
47 – Percentage of people in a recent test that stopped to help an attractive woman who had dropped a stack of papers in a NYC street.
94 – Percentage of men who don't really see anything wrong with that.

The Lycoming Affair

Insipid blathering by Dan Marvin

Up in the wispy thinness of inner space, just between the layers called home by clouds and those inhabited by vacuum, live the pluralflues. To call them thin is to not really understand two dimensions. Covering an atomic thickness in one direction and hundreds of square miles in the others, the pluralflues never stood up for themselves. They drifted, some would say mindlessly, day in and day out. They also stretched the limits of what might be considered life since they spontaneously formed, lived pretty much forever, and didn't talk a whole lot. In all, they led a serene if not particularly interesting existence.

Occasionally, one would overlap another and they would have a short conversation. Broadly interpreted, a pluralflue chat would sound something like "Are you?" "I am." "Am I?" "You are." It was either deeply philosophical or utter nonsense, but they would continue on like that until the barely perceptible winds pulled them apart again. The great oral traditions of the pluralflue could be accurately recorded on a postcard to be saved for posterity.

One decade, an odd thing happened. Several of the pluralflue ceased to be. ("Are they?" "They aren't." "Were they?" "They were.") One decade they were swimming in the ozone over the poles and the next decade they weren't. This, not surprisingly, caused a flurry of concern in the pluralflue community. Many theories were offered for their disappearance ("No more?" "No more") but nothing concrete was ever found to explain the sudden reduction in their numbers. They drifted and grumbled.

Other odd things began to crop up as well. Projectiles began to lift off from the surface of the planet and rip through an unsuspecting pluralflue on a regular, if sporadic, basis. They were used to things sometimes coming down from on top, and had developed a system of sorts for determining when this was going to happen and made sure not to be there. When the projectiles came from below, however, it was impossible to predict their presence until after they had passed through one of them. This was painful indeed. ("Ow?" "Cripes!")

As they drifted, occasionally talking, the pluralflues began to suspect that some influence from the planet's surface was causing their problems. It was hard for a two dimensional being to envision what a surface of anything might be like, but they could sense the increase in temperature from below, they could sense odd chemicals in the mix, and they had direct proof that something was shooting at them.

As they had done millions of years before, the pluralflue became opaque, reflecting the sun instead of letting it through. They didn't know why it worked, but eventually the projectiles stopped, the air below them cooled, and they resumed their mindless drifting, once again unmolested by the upstart 'intelligence' below.

The End

Dick

Contemporary fiction by Dan Marvin

He slumped low in the seat of the Buick, a baseball cap covering his eyes. He could have been asleep, but he wasn't. He was watching. In the seat next to him, an empty Dunkin Donuts box gave mute testimony to just how long he had been waiting. The constant call of his bladder added some emphasis, if she didn't come home soon; he'd be taking a leak in the service station across the way when she did show up for sure.

For Andy Proehl, the road from idealistic do-gooder to paid snoop had been a fairly short fall. As the excitement of helping others had slowly succumbed to the excitement of opening a new bottle of Jack Daniels, his standards of what constituted a career were similarly adjusted. Within 15 years of heading off to college he was a failed out lawyer, a used to be husband, and an erstwhile private eye. His fees were reasonable and his discretion unquestioned, so he got work. Most of it involved sitting in a Buick with an empty box of Dunkin Donuts, watching his hair fall out in the rearview mirror.

Finally he gave in to nature, dashing for the convenience shop to give back 32 oz of rented coffee. As he came out, wiping his hands on a damp brown square of paper towel, he heard the growl of the engine coming up the street. With a well chosen expletive, he headed for the front seat of the Buick and made it just in time to push his hat down, pick his camera up, and pretend to be asleep while his heart pounded a mile a minute.

The car was old, not what he was expecting. Instead of a Jaguar or a Ferrari, Mrs. Ned Campbell was being chauffeured around in a 1992 Ford Taurus. It had a few rust spots on the trunk, missing a wheel cover as if that could detract from the faded gold paint. She obviously wasn't out for fun with a flashy guy. He readied his camera and got a shot of the license, Jimmy at the squad house still owed him one and he might collect if he couldn't find out who the guy was any other way.

Even across the street, he heard her laughing. It was her, of course, just where Mr. Ned Campbell had told him to look. Why he'd hired a private eye was beyond him, with a day off work and something resembling guts, Ned could have had his wife back for free. Oh well, Andy wasn't an idealist, more of a pragmatist. Just because Ned's hand was limp when he shook and he clearly had better things to do than talk to the hired help was no reason that Andy should get soft.

The laugh caught him off guard though. He wasn't expecting... happy. Clandestine perhaps, maybe a little giddy at the prospect of getting away with something that she really wasn't getting away with. But happy caught him off guard; he wasn't sure what to make of it. He flashed a picture of her as she laughed, she was oblivious to him, and all she could see was the man getting out holding the door for her. He wasn't much to look at honestly. A bit overweight, casual clothes that needed ironing before they went into the suitcase. Still, he looked at her like a commoner might view a Princess; his eyes were alight with her. Andy flashed another picture as they kissed. Just like that, he had it. He watched them until he held the door for her and bowed gallantly, and she crossed the threshold regally, the man following her in without the slightest trace of suspicion that Andy Proehl had just made his life a lot more interesting.

Andy waited until the shades in apartment 1F dropped down, then he started the Buick, threw the empty Dunkin Donuts box out the window, and headed back to his office. He hustled the camera upstairs and stepped into the dark room. He was amazed as he watched her develop; he hadn't realized how beautiful she truly was. Certainly some of it was the smile, her face alight when she laughed. But there was quality there too, a sense that all was right in the world as long as you were looking at her. He developed the first picture, then the second... then the one of them kissing. She shut her eyes, Andy noticed, but the man didn't. He wanted to be looking while he could.

When all was said and done, there were 6 pictures. Two of them involved things that a married woman who wanted to survive a messy divorce proceeding probably shouldn't be doing with a man not her husband. Andy looked at the pictures until he'd memorized her features. Could a quality woman like that ever really be expected to be faithful to Ned Campbell? Could a man who shook hands like he was shaking with a dead fish and probably ignored this glorious creature ever really deserve her? Andy didn't think so.

The phone broke him out of his reverie. "Andy, Ned Campbell here. Did you get the shots?" The voice was whiny on the phone, demanding but unsure all at once.

"Yep, sure did! Come on over and you can have them." Andy answered immediately. His opportunity to be the knight in shining armor for a beautiful woman he'd never have slipping inevitably away with one more completed assignment.

The End

Erroneous Excerpt – "Checkest me out, I'm the King. This be way cool, anon. Bringest me some dinner, methinks beef tonight, and wine! All of this death has maketh me way hungry."

Hamlet II – Fortinbras the Hungry William Shakespeare

Distress

Watered down fiction by Dan Marvin

It was official, Reginald was in trouble. He'd been taking on water for about half an hour, at least to any serious degree. The bilge pumps had been running non-stop, it was becoming obvious that the jolt he had felt earlier in the afternoon was more than just the wind catching the sails in another direction, he had a leak.

Whereas most men would probably have started to panic, Reginald sat his seasoned bottom down on a seat in the stern and assessed his options, a black stemmed pipe clutched in his teeth, smoke quickly dissipating into the increasingly windy salt air. It had been a gift from his daughter, a lifetime ago. He appreciated it most because she didn't like the fact that he smoked, didn't approve of his vice, but respected her father enough to make sure he enjoyed it just the same. It was a completely selfless gift from a completely terrific daughter.

His life had been a good one. In the few minutes of reflection he indulged himself, he thought back to the wonderful redheaded woman that had never let him wonder "what if", the daughter that they had raised, and then the son they hadn't expected but loved just the same. He thought about 35 years of friendships made with people that understood that he'd never be there forever, but just for now was good enough. Also he thought about the sea, that churning gray enigma that even now threatened to swallow him up. The boat was starting to groan beneath him, his last chance for peaceful reflection was just about up.

Resignedly, he sent out the distress call. It would be automatically picked up by receivers somewhere, relayed to vessels somewhere else. Unless he was extremely lucky, the signal would only serve to pinpoint where to search for his remains. He inflated the life raft, made sure the provisions were stowed, and left it on the deck. Only then did he go down below to assess the damage. He had been methodical his whole life, it had been his salvation, up to this point at least.

The break was there, of course, just below the waterline. Well below the waterline now, actually. He had honestly thought it would be worse, although it was bad enough. There was no point in trying to stuff anything into the rift; he had to come up with a better plan. The pumps continued in the background, getting further and further behind as the boat began to list to the starboard. He had to think quickly.

He was going into the water anyway, he reckoned, and the sea wasn't that bad at the moment. He quickly set about getting on his diving mask and oxygen canisters. He looked around and found a stout cookie tin, large enough to cover the hole. Hammer and nails were next, it would be very difficult to operate under water but he had to try. He dropped over the side into a boiling world of waves and surf. It was hard just getting to the boat, almost impossible to steady himself enough to work on it.

His fingers clawed at the cookie sheet to bend it into shape. The suction created by the water flowing into the hole was pretty effective at keeping it there. Now came the real challenge, somehow pounding it on without doing more damage. The first two nails were quickly wasted; he'd have to do better. His son's eyes floated in front of him somehow, eyes faded and gray just like his own, eyes that were wiser than his had been at that age. The image gave him another thought, he gouged the metal with the claws of the hammer itself in several spots, and then the nails went in easier. The sea tossed him about with the ship, banging him into it painfully more than once. Still, it was the only way. He tried hard not to think about sharks.

Finally he had one of the nails in. His arms ached and rebelled, he was no longer a young seaman. Another nail made it, things were looking better. A third made it through the cookie sheet and into the hull, better still. He was thankful that he'd insisted on wood for the hull. Maybe a composite wouldn't have broken when he hit whatever it was, but he certainly wouldn't be nailing into it now if it had. A fourth nail let him breath easier, at least figuratively. He was starting to gasp for breath in the mask, he checked and his tank had less than five minutes left. There were no other tanks, nor did his arms feel especially strong. One more nail would have to do. He reached into his pocket and found... nothing. No more nails. Desperately he almost tore the pocket off of his shirt, then tried his pants. There in his left pocket he found one last nail. He almost lost it when a big wave crashed over them, then it was started, then it was in. He came up to the surface with no air left, gasping for air and swimming for the ladder.

He held on for a long time, a tired old man who had fought a terrific battle. He held onto the bottom step and bobbed up and down with the boat. He could feel the vibration of the pumps, still gamely mopping up for him. Most of all, he could sense her pulse again, a pulse that he had felt sure was gone for good. Finally he clamored back over onto the deck, walked over his life raft, and went below.

Hours later, he had rested a bit, cleaned up a bit more, and canceled the alert. The seal was holding for now, it wouldn't hold forever but hopefully it would last until he could get to port. He sat down at the terminal and brought up the screen... there was a note from his daughter. "Daddy" it began. "I just wanted you to be the first one to hear the news. I'm pregnant! Roger is so excited, he's already talking about what colour to paint the baby's room. If it's a boy, I'm naming it after you!" Somehow the patch would hold, it had to.

The End

Authors Note – this is the longest story in the collection, I hope you saved it for a time when no one is knocking and asking when you're going to be done, already.

ReDick

Abstract art in the form of fiction by Dan Marvin

Mrs. Ned Campbell had been haunting him a little lately. Andy Proehl hated to think he might be developing a conscience, but he didn't like the way the whole thing had ended. The pictures had been incriminating enough; she was caught in the act. Her husband had paid him enough, a bit more than he had asked actually. It should have been easy, but it wasn't.

Probably the worst things were the pictures he hadn't taken. The ones of her on the front of the Social pages, trying to shade her pretty face from the camera-man, serving only to look guiltier to an already jaded public. None of the story was about the way the other man had looked at her, about the happiness that he gave her that Ned Campbell obviously couldn't. No, the story was about how Ned regretted having to go through with it but was going to have to divorce his wife of 15 years, how his wife had been caught with another man and how he just couldn't bare the lies.

In truth, Andy doubted she'd ever lied one way or the other. He doubted that Ned Campbell asked his wife where she was going on a Wednesday evening, all dressed up for dinner. He doubted that he cared much when the garage door closed at 3AM and she went to sleep in the other room. Andy had gotten called to the witness stand, since it was he who had taken the pictures. He hadn't liked looking out and seeing her there, looking very distinguished but a whole lot less happy. Seeing her eyes looking pained and knowing that he'd caused it had created a bit of the feeling gnawing away at his gut now. It almost felt like guilt.

He was shocked when the knock at his door turned into Mrs. Ned Campbell. Actually, the former Mrs. Ned Campbell. He scrambled out of his chair and looked to see if any hired thugs were following her in but they weren't. She was alone. "Sit down Mr. Proehl, you and I have to talk." Andy sat down.

"I know that you took the pictures that my husband used in court. I went through a period where I really hated you for that." She was very matter of fact; it left him with nothing to do save nodding in agreement. "Then I realized that you were just doing what Ned hired you to do. So now I have a job for you." At that, Andy raised his eyebrows.

"Really Mrs. Camp..." she cut him off. "Call me Rosetta. Like the stone." "Very well, Rosetta. I can't take your case, it would be a conflict of interest." He said the words but wasn't real convinced of them himself. He was a hired fact gatherer, it didn't really matter who the facts were about or for.

"I saw how you couldn't look at me in the courtroom, or couldn't look at me for very long. You didn't like Ned and felt very uncomfortable to be caught in the middle of it. I'm giving you a chance to redeem yourself, Mr. Proehl." She was looking over the desk at him in a way that made him want to be redeemed.

"Call me Andy, please. And yes, everything you're saying is accurate. It seemed like some easy cash, your husband gave me the location and the time and you showed up like clockwork. But when I was developing the pictures, I knew that I didn't have the whole story. You really love him, don't you? The other man, I mean."

"That's not really part of the conversation." For the first time, she looked a little unsure of herself. "I want you to take some pictures for me this time. The judge hasn't decided on custody or alimony just yet, I'd like a few pictures of my own to tip the scale a bit more in my favor." With that, she laid out the plan and Andy Proehl was pretty much speechless.

It was another stakeout, another set of pictures. He really should have begged off on this one, given a chance for Louis Smantz to pick up a case with a well placed referral. Instead, he was back in the Buick, camera at the ready, and waiting. Unlike his wife, Ned was more punctual. He was also more perverted. The young man he was walking with seemed very interested in Ned, more so than Rosetta would likely be ever again. Andy's camera whirred away as they strolled hand in hand down the street. Having him holding hands with another man wouldn't be enough though, and Andy really didn't want to think about what was coming next.

They slipped inside the house and Andy waited for a few minutes for them to get comfortable. He then took his camera and walked around to the back of the place, there were plenty of bushes and no lights. Again, it was a pretty easy job. He tried hard to focus on the documentation and not the act but he left with a slightly upset stomach and a definite decision for this to his last task for either of the Campbells.

Rosetta stopped by the next day and registered no surprise at the pictures, no reaction of any kind. Instead, she paid Andy his $250, and actually kissed him on the cheek. "You did the right thing" she whispered before she left. Andy wasn't really sure any more.

The End

Questionable Quotation – "Two roads diverged in a wood and I... I took the one less traveled by... Of extra work I'm not a fan... I was looking for the can" - Jack Frost

Blind Luck

Literate lunacy by Dan Marvin

It was third and long at the 23 yard line when I went up to catch the pass. It was a well thrown ball, out in front of me where I could catch it in stride. It hit me right in the numbers and I didn't let go of it. I held onto it when my head caught on fire. I held on when the ground came up to meet me hard. I held onto it when I couldn't feel my fingers anymore. I held onto it when the trainers came out on the field and told me to let go of it. I held onto it as they loaded me onto the backboard, then onto the cart, the fans cheering listlessly and worried about me. Not half as worried as I was. I'd only gained 8 yards, we needed nine.

The first night in the hospital was surreal. I wasn't one of those lucky players that have a devoted wife and 3 beautiful kids to worry and stew. I was one of the guys that stays out late and flirts with the waitresses at Hooters and gets his name in the paper for fighting with a dumb drunk guy in a bar downtown. Not evil, just young. Young with too much money and too few friends. On this particular night, no friends. The rest of the team had trooped in after the game, a 23-10 loss, but then they'd hopped on an airplane and headed back home and I was stuck in a hospital in a town I didn't know surrounded by no one at all. My agent wasn't there; I didn't really expect him to be. My family wasn't there; they lived 1400 miles away and were frantically making plane reservations but wouldn't be here until the next afternoon. Nope, it was just me, and my little machine that beeped in time with my heartbeat and the nurses who occasionally came in to write something on my chart or see if I needed to move my bowels. The worst part was, I really had no idea, and I couldn't feel them.

The x-rays had come back inconclusive. I had no idea what that meant, I thought if a bone was broken the x-rays either showed it or they didn't. No one had ever mentioned the third possibility, inconclusive. It was the worst possibility really, at least initially. The team doctor was there, he looked everything over and nodded dourly as he talked to the physician on call at the hospital and they decided to keep me under observation that night and pump me full of some drugs that might help if my spine was injured which certainly seemed to be the case. The hospital got quiet and the adrenaline wore off and the nurse turned off the beeps and I started to doze off even though I couldn't move.

The itching cut into my dreams. In my dream I was surrounded by spider webs. Everywhere I walked, I ran into more and more until I couldn't move and it was itchy and the spider was closing in. In reality, I was itchy. I opened my eyes and focused on the clock on the TV, it read 4:40 AM. The hospital was really quiet; I didn't have any idea if itchy was good. Still, it felt like something so I took it as a good sign and slept off and on until breakfast arrived.

The itching was spreading, down my left side. The doctor came in that morning and poked me with needles. The day before, I hadn't been able to feel a damn thing. That morning, though, I could feel it down almost to my waist. He smiled a big smile and told me to squeeze his hand and my fingers bent a little. It wasn't a death grip, but it certainly might have been a life grip. Later on, I had to go to the bathroom. And I knew it.

By the time my family trooped in, I was sitting up and sipping some soup. The soup wasn't that wonderful, but the fact that I could sit up and sip it was. I wiggled my toes for them because they seemed most interested in seeing that. Hell, I was more than willing to show off my toe wiggling skill. There were careful hugs around, and my agent called in and the PR guy for the team called in and everyone seemed genuinely happy that I could wiggle my toes.

Two weeks later, I was back in the starting lineup at wide receiver. My coach certainly hoped that I could do a lot more than wiggle my toes. I did too. I stood up after the first hit, ball still in my hands and feeling my whole body. First down...

The End

Erroneous Excerpt – "The White Whale swam before him as the monomaniac incarnation of all those malicious agencies which some deep men feel eating in them, till they are left living on with half a heart and half a lung and half a spleen and half a kidney and two thirds of a liver and three quarters of a large intestine and a little over a third of a gall bladder."

Moby Organ - Melville

Deaf Date

"It's a play on words" Hebron said, trying to keep the exasperation out of his voice. Humor is never better when you have to explain it. He could tell from the blank look on her face that she still didn't get it, that she'd never get it, but she laughed gamely and went back to her salad. Would she never eat a real meal? Why did he have to keep buying $20 salads that she picked at? She could actually use to gain a few pounds.

The conversation had obviously peaked, she didn't offer up any scintillating tidbits. He tried to fill the void with conversation about what she had done at work that day, the details weren't forthcoming. Pulling teeth might have been more enjoyable. He nodded sympathetically as she haltingly told him about someone at work that he'd never met, how much she disliked this girl, how this girl knew everything and she knew nothing, and secretly Hebron wondered if the other girl at work was a babe.

"What do you want to do after dinner?" The last date he had planned an elaborate chain of events, all predicated on the idea that she would want to go out and spend some time with him after dinner. She'd neglected to tell him that she wanted to go to bed early for some unspecified reason. He'd assumed that it was the end of the 'relationship' but was shocked when she called and sounded hurt that he'd never called her back. This date he wanted to make more casual, to leave some loose ends.

"Oh, I don't know, what do you like to do?" It hinted at conversation, at curiosity, but she immediately went back to her salad and red wine even as he was answering. She nodded dully, almost like she was listening, but he doubted that she heard his love of swing music, how there was a great swing club an easy cab ride or slightly harder walk down the street, how he'd love to introduce her to his friends. "That's nice." What a gal.

They did do the swing club, although he probably should have figured out that it would be similarly dismal. The music was great, the atmosphere low key and romantic, but she was impervious to it all. Yes, she ordered a martini, but if she took two sips of the $7 concoction he'd be shocked. It sat there, slowly warming as the band played on and the rest of the bar talked and laughed together. They discussed her cats until the band took a break.

Finally they made their way back to his car, he held the door for her and she got up the gumption to mumble 'thank you' before tipping her head back drowsily against the headrest. She must be on some heavy duty painkillers or something, Hebron conjectured. Last stop, her apartment. He dutifully opened the door and walked her to the portal, expecting a peck on the cheek and a good night.

She surprised him by pulling him by the lapels and searching his mouth with her tongue. "Want to come in for some dessert?" She asked, suddenly wide awake. "Y..yes!" He stammered, Hebron was in love...

The End

The Fox and the 4x4

Contemporary fiction by Dan Marvin

From beneath the trees came the excited rustle of rabbits, Eunisia sensed that they had found a rather tasty patch of clover. She was sensitive, for a skunk, and left the rabbits to their fun. In one sense, being a skunk was a delightful existence, you were left largely on your own and could come and go as you pleased. On a slightly more personal level though, it was often a lonely life, even other skunks didn't come for tea regularly.

Eunisia waddled into a patch of nearby flowers, she rarely did anything quickly, and nature usually cut her a fairly wide path. The bees didn't really notice her defenses, of course, and the birds were pretty immune to her charms, but the deer and more importantly, the predators knew that picking on Eunisia was a good way to get a face full of stink. She dug up some tasty roots and enjoyed them thoroughly.

Ahead she heard a scuffle breaking out, the rabbits streaked by her, heading undoubtedly back to their warren. Some other animal was up there and obviously on the losing side of a debate. She listened to hear if it was someone she knew, the meadow was a pretty familiar place after three years. She couldn't place a voice, but the urgent tone of its owner left her wondering whether to investigate or head the other way. When she heard the strident rumble of the fox's voice, she decided on option two.

The grasses of the meadow parted before her, she could sense that she had attracted the attention of the fox as the altercation behind her ended and the soft paw pads rustled in the grass behind her. She was looking for a good place to make a stand, somewhere without as much vegetation to disperse her pungent liquid. Up ahead she could see a clearing, there, that would do nicely.

Eunisia stopped and lifted her tail; she knew that the fox would be there in moments. A red nose stuck out from the bushes "I'm going to eat you little princess" the fox snarled, his thin voice trailing off into a yip of excitement. The wind shifted though and his look turned from anticipation to concern. "What is that smell?"

With a smile, Eunisia replied "Why, it's the smell of how I'd taste, mighty hunter. Perhaps the rabbits would be more to your liking." The fox turned in place once, perplexed by how this was going. He certainly didn't like how it smelled.

The F150 rounded the corner and didn't even have time to brake; Eunisia's vaunted defenses were no match for its shear tonnage. The fox did get a faceful, but he decided it could have been much worse as he watched her twitch on the road and lie still. Admiringly, he watched the much larger predator through stinging eyes. If only he had one of those...

The End

Reverie

Introspection by Dan Marvin

Long after the flames had turned into embers, he sat on the log, staring into the glowing coals but seeing his life. This was where he felt the most calm, the most relaxed, yet even here he wondered. The smell of wood smoke, the lingering taste of a couple of brews, these didn't really intrude on his consciousness. The stress of his job, the argument with his wife, the growing list of issues with his kids, these made a cameo appearance instead. Maybe it was just because it was quiet there in the woods. Maybe the beer had mellowed him out and let him think, let his mind wander. Whatever the reason, his life flowed by him now in an unending parade of images.

He relived how he'd left his last job, not really voluntarily. He supposed he still had unresolved issues over that one. He thought flittingly about how he missed his dad, even after all these years. Psychiatrists would have to work hard to compete with Keystone Light tonight. Mostly, he thought about if this is where he really wanted to be, all things considered.

It wasn't a bad life. If you'd asked him 20 years ago to speculate on where he'd be right now, he probably wouldn't have pictured the wealth of material goods, good friends, and slightly erratic path to where he now lived. Even his marriage and kids were a testament to surviving the odds, certainly not perfect but not so bad either. There was warmth and laughter there from time to time, even among the frustrations of day to day living. What part of his soul still felt empty? Would it ever feel full?

A log shifted and some sparks flew up into the night. In the distance, a small animal rustled in the underbrush. A fish smacked at a fly on the pond, loud enough to break into his reverie for a moment. He breathed in the rapidly chilling air, looked up at the sky, strewn with a glittering carpet of stars. He liked it out here, not so much light and noise as his 'real' life. In the cabin were a couple of buddies, already gone to sleep, worn out from the 101 things they had to get done to get a 'free' night out.

He heard someone stirring; perhaps he wasn't the only one of the three awake. The door opened, a slice of light fell across the ground and then was extinguished as the door closed again. "Dude, I brought you a beer. Let's go skinny dipping." Their clothes hit the ground and they hit the pond, reverie broken by the more pressing need to get really cold and do something stupid.

The End

Curse of the Bat People

A fictional curse by Dan Marvin

He came into being as little more than a speck, a bit of dust belched from an ancient volcano, flung into the air. Around him coalesced microscopic droplets of water, each one serving to build him up, making him larger and larger until he started to feel a mysterious pull, one that he had resisted all his life. With a silent shout, he began to fall, leaving behind the nursery of the cloud, riding the wind with billions of his siblings, falling ever faster towards the swiftly approaching ground below.

It was almost the end, a sickening splat as he hit a tree leaf. The lights went out for what seemed like a long time but must have been only a few moments. When he came too, he was already building back up, the tree leaf funneling tiny rivulets of water towards him, making him larger again. At last he broke the resolve of the leaf, it bent downward and he felt the now-familiar sensation of flight, much shorter this time. He impacted a hard, glass surface and almost immediately a rubber squeegee send him careening to his left. There was no hesitation this time, when he hit he was already starting to rush, the road swept by with increasing velocity until he cannonballed through the grating and into the darkness.

Below the ride became increasingly turbulent, through a series of ancient conduits he rode with his brothers, their body now fully a stream. Ahead there was light, and he rushed out of the sluice, riding a roller coaster of rocks until he found himself riding the rapids. Wheeee! It was fun, he helped kick up foam as he swirled past the submerged snags and headed helter-skelter towards whatever fate had in store for him.

The adrenaline didn't last long, although the calmer waters of the river gave him more time to reflect. He gave up his heat energy and sank, the bottom of the river was cold and dark. He was happy when other water flushed him back upwards, he could feel the sun start to warm him again as he returned on the slow moving ride. And so it went for awhile, bobbing and sinking, occasionally catching on a log or a branch them moving ahead again with a whirl. It was hard to tell when one river stopped and the next began, he only felt the sense of being connected with a larger and larger mass.

He sensed the salt before he got to the ocean; the water became bitter with it as the tide fought with the current of the mighty river. He was curious about the ocean, so different than his journey so far. He had picked up some elements on his way, tore off some atoms of heavy metals and pesticides but he had never felt the concentration of anything the way he felt the sodium and potassium starting to make his molecules swell. With a final look back he was loose in the ocean, becoming more saline.

If the river had a cycle, the ocean positively had a current. He moved this way and that based on the undeniable hand of energy. Some was caused by the moon, some by the temperature, some by the sun, some by the propeller of a passing freighter. He spent time in the depths, bummed out by the darkness and caving in under the pressure, only to find light once more when fate smiled on him in the form of an eyeless fish who needed his minimal reserves of oxygen more than he did. He gave them up and got a ride back upward as his reward.

As he approached the surface, the sun warmed him, it felt good, it felt... liberating. It WAS liberating, he had been liberated from the surface of the ocean altogether! Up up he went, little more than a vapor now but enjoying the floating sensation. He could see the clouds waiting for him, ready to embrace him once more... he was coming home.

The End

Phabricated Philosophy – When you look out the window, are you sure it's not just a big TV installed by aliens to show you what they want you to see? Yes, you can walk outside! And then hope it's not just a big holographic image created by aliens to show you what they want you to see.

Desert Winds

Back to the high life by Dan Marvin

He sat his horse with a loose-jointed gracefulness that belied years on the trail. Beneath his legs, the dapple twitched his tail and then dropped his head to munch on some tender looking grass that was in short supply in this part of the world. Londo looked at the sun blasted terrain ahead, squinting his eyes to try to make out dust that could mean men. Or Indians. He saw neither, and no sound drifted up to him. With a flick of the reins, the dapple started forward, moving down off of the hill and further into the unknown.

The trail was like thousands of others in this part of the world, most likely carved by game as they moved through the low lying brush looking for food and water. Since it was a trail, there were probably water holes, but they would be hidden and not easily found. His bedroll contained a change of clothes and some basic provisions but nothing that would last him for an extended period of time here in hell. And yet, he had a job to do, the bullet hole in his sleeve and the thin sliver of blood it had produced on his forearm were stinging reminders that he had a debt to pay.

Two days before, the thought of crossing the desert was far from his mind. He had been working the Bar S for almost two years, making $30 a month and spending little of it, trying to save enough to start his own spread soon. The trouble had started without warning; a shot from cover dropped the boss as he went to get water from the well. The three hands that had been in the bunkhouse asleep had been pinned down and killed as well. By the time Londo rode back in from his watch, the festivities were almost over. Almost. He had seen the body lying in the dust from a fair ways off and cut off the path immediately to think things over.

He'd liked the boss, a tough Texan who had turned 100 head into a working ranch with the help of some guys that Londo also liked. Now his blood was leaking back into the Texas soil that had flowered under his oversight and the Bar S was in the control of ... someone. Someone Londo didn't know but soon would have to face. It wasn't in him to back off, to ride away, this was personal. Plus his $347 was in that bunkhouse, hidden under a loose board with loving care, and the bunkhouse was now in enemy hands.

That had been two days ago, and on his back-trail were two men who thought they were quick on the draw and one that really was but had been unlucky. He had his $347 tied to the pommel of his saddle, and one more man to find. That man was the leader, and right now he was out there, somewhere. His dapple had an uncommon love of roaming, and he set off at a rapid clip.

His horse kicked up dust and he ate it, the alkali tasting salty on his lips. He moved his bandana over his mouth as his face slowly turned dust brown. After an hour he did see some dust on the horizon, instead of chasing it he found some high ground to have a better look. One man, on a horse, making tracks. The dapple responded to the touch of the spurs and headed out with renewed vigor. He came over the rise and was almost knocked off his horse as the spaceship chose that moment to rise from its hiding place and float just over the surface of the desert. He watched in awe at the shiny saucer, the sunshine seemingly being absorbed into its surface, the dancing lights visible even in the midday sun. Somewhere out there, another set of eyes was watching too, eyes that had some explaining to do. As the space ship continued to glide, Londo urged his horse forward to find those eyes...

The End

Erroneous Excerpt – "My fellow Americans, I come before you today because things are pretty great right now, there aren't any major crisis' at the moment and we don't need to raise taxes or anything. Really I just wanted to say hi, let you know I'm here doing my job, and now I'll send you back to the 'Price is Right'

- No President, ever

Time wave

Time for some fiction by Dan Marvin

The wall meandered through the meadow, a current reminder of years long passed when men had time to cull rocks from the fields and stack them in a row that went on and on and on. Here and there a few rocks had tumbled, mute testament to the blunderings of animals or men or trees. In the crevices, spiders and other critters found a home, moss grew with abandon, and the slow process of entropy continued to turn the stones back into dust.

If you viewed the wall from a distance, it pointed to a barn that still stood with the help of some braces that arrived long after it had outlived its original design. The wood was gray, the color of a leaden sky during a late summer rain storm. In truth, it had survived more of these rain storms than the builder would have anticipated, coming out on the other side a little more battered, but undeterred in its determination to stay erect. Eventually, even determination wouldn't be enough but for now, it was winning. Or at least coming to a draw.

South of the old barn, past the rusty ruins of a tractor that had long since made its last furrow in the overgrown fields, just down the grass covered lane, was a farmhouse. The siding was still white, just less white than it had been originally as the color came off in chalky streaks in the rain, running through the downspouts and into the creek beside it. The windows and doors looked a bit like a face, as though the house was permanently puckered into a look of derision at the folly of man.

Whereas time at the barn and the fence continued forward, time inside the house stood still. The furniture was locked firmly in the 70's; vinyl chairs with cigarette scars the predominant decorating feature. Through doors that didn't quite close all the way, past closets of clothes that once had been comfortable, sat a man. He didn't feel the presence of the clothes or the doors or the wall, he wasn't really there. His body was there, but his attention was elsewhere, always elsewhere.

He watched the flickering blue screen with active, interested eyes. It had been years since those eyes beheld the house or the barn or the fence with that much interest, maybe never. Now they watched the characters parading across the message box in rapid succession, now they looked at the keyboard as he typed in his response, now they darted back to the screen. The age of the rugged outdoorsman continued to slowly evolve into the age of the not so rugged indoorsman…

The End

Driving Mr. Smith

Contemplative fiction by Dan Marvin

Stashed neatly in the boot of the car, like a bundle of groceries, was Sir Robert Condrate Smith. Typically a Thursday night such as this, with its sticky heat and thin, hazy moonlight would find him safely ensconced at home, perhaps puffing on a cigar with a snifter of brandy. This particular Thursday night, however, found him rocketing about London in the boot of a car not designed to contain his considerable girth, and in an advanced state of despair.

The evening had started out routinely enough, he had walked the greyhounds through Hampstead Heath, watching the anglers going about their business with rods and reels and wondering if the fish to be had there were truly worth the effort. Sometimes the pursuit of the thing was more valuable than the thing itself, he supposed. The dogs had done their business and in homage to 21st century sensibility he had picked the steaming piles up in a plastic bag and deposited them in yet another, larger plastic bag, insulating them for eternity against the natural forces that would have soon turned them into greener grass. Ah, progress.

The walk had ended with Sir Robert Condrate Smith looking decidedly winded, and the greyhounds looking decidedly ready to continue along without him. Nonetheless, he unleashed them in the mud room and went about preparing his supper. Tins of salmon on toast points with mint and a small salad were followed with a sensible portion of scotch. When his appetites were sated, he settled in at his desk to work on his books. He had no sooner opened the ledger when a hood was placed unceremoniously over his balding pate. His attempts at screams were decidedly muffled, and his attempts at freedom were similarly thwarted with quickly rendered knots. He was speedily trussed and stuffed into the boot before either Sir Robert Condrate Smith or any of his nosy neighbors were any the wiser. As the days unfolded they would undoubtedly hear of his disappearance, but none of them would have the ultimate conversational trump card of having SEEN the thing. He rather despised his neighbors.

Now, as the car sped through the winding streets, he lost all sense of direction. He struggled vainly to hear the wail of a following siren, all he heard was the road and the horns and the impatience of evening traffic. What could they possibly want with him? Ransom? Certainly the former Madame Robert Condrate Smith would chuckle merrily if it was suggested that she pay for his return, his departure from her life would not dampen her spirits in the least. His parents were dead; there were no children from his loveless and ill-fated marriage. No, it couldn't be for ransom. Had he made anyone angry recently? Not to the extent that this retaliation would be called for, it was an uncivilized escalation of any business related transgressions. In short, he drew a blank as he rattled around and thumped his head and generally cursed the unreliability of greyhounds as guard dogs.

At long last, the mystery vehicle ground to a stop, its brakes protesting their part in the plot with mechanical squeals. He expected to be accosted by hostile hands at any moment, but the car doors slammed and then there was just nothing. Nothing for a long time. His arms began aching from the fetters, the ropes unpleasantly taut. He was sweating into the bag over his head; the night had succeeded only in getting darker, not less dank. Finally, as his adrenaline started to retreat and he began to doze, the lid opened quietly and he was grabbed by rough hands. They dragged him forward, up some steps, helped him duck his head but not before he bumped it rather badly, and plopped him in a chair. The ropes were loosened but not removed, and the hood was yanked quickly off. He saw only light, blinding light, and he blinked his eyes against it. In the darkness beyond the light, a voice began to speak.... "Oh drat, you're not him. Terribly sorry old chap, I'll have Lou drive you back. So hard to find good help these days." Dumbly, Sir Robert Condrate Smith nodded, then the hood was placed back over his head, and he was once again spirited off to the boot of the car for the round trip portion of his journey.

The End

Dubious Definition – Vacillate – What happens when you don't vacil in time.

The Icy Hand of Fate

Oddly formatted fiction by Dan Marvin

Sunlight dripped through the leaves like raindrops in the wind when the storm is passed, splashing with brilliant yellow force on the mossy logs below. The twitter of unseen birds overhead competed with the stirring of last year's leaves to catch the ear. An earthy smell of new life growing through the remains of old life wafted up with every step and the breeze whispered through the newly green leaves, chilly with the reminder of a winter perhaps not yet passed.

In the shadow of a fallen log, hidden away from all but the sharpest eyes, Quino surveyed the seemingly peaceful scene. At his scale, the world was a much scarier place. Friends and relatives had been lost to the ever vigilant winged hunters above, and others had become meals for scavengers below. But Quino had to eat, and eating required movement. Movement begat danger. Eat he must, and off he scampered.

Over a knoll, around a sapling, rooting through the detritus from innumerable trees, Quino found a treat. One of last years acorns, still bearing its precious cargo! He took time for a brief celebratory chitter before grabbing it up and heading back to his hollow log. The sound caught the ear of the young Ekere, a red fox with a luxurious tail and the impetuous insolence of youth. He started to give chase, but was restrained by Levant, his father. "Be patient my son. You cannot chase a sound. Wait until you see your quarry." Ekere hunkered down, waiting, vigilant.

The birds were silent, perhaps they sensed the hunters' presence, or perhaps they were napping from getting up early chasing worms. Whatever the cause, the only sound was the breeze rustling the leaves. Ekere waited, watching, vigilant. Although Quino hadn't seen the hunters, somehow an ingrained sense of danger kept him still, kept him quiet. It was a standoff as deadly as any at the OK corral.

Time passed. Ekere grew impatient, bored. He wanted to leave, wanted to find other easier food but Levant was there, and Levant had said to be patient. Patient was tough when you were young! From nowhere, Quino attacked, his needle sharp teeth sinking deep into Ekere's flank. Other teeth found equally tender spots; Ekere twisted, turned, barked and whined trying to shake off the tiny aggressors. "Run my son!" Levant led the retreat through the underbrush and Ekere followed, panicked, the chipmunks grudgingly falling away as he sped off. In the sun dappled glen, Quino did his victory lap and, as luck would have it, found another acorn in the process.

The End

The Unwitting Hero

Fiction for the florist in your life by Dan Marvin

The last vestige of flame licked at the mostly burned logs, brown bark long since turned into white ash with a few red embers. The fire threw off a flicker of light but not much heat. There was no one left standing to tend to it, the drunken snores of partiers could be heard in the thin, cold air. The rustling of a nocturnal creature was the only sound that stirred in accompaniment to the last cracklings of the fire.

It was one of those last cracklings that helped the spark make its escape. It popped free from the rest of the log and came to rest on a leaf. It was ravenous; needing to burn... it heated the leaf until it succumbed, a thin pale flame working out in a circle from the ember. The flame found strength in its dryness and encouraged another leaf to join it in burning. Between the two of them, they produced a stronger light, and more heat.

Nearby, a stick longed to be part of the party. It crackled a bit as it burst into flame itself, first the thinnest part of its length but later the thicker part as well. Like the leaf, it had a friend and the friend wanted in on the action. The friend was a bigger stick that lay on top of it. The bigger stick had more substance and it got quite hot. The leaves that had fallen on top of the bigger stick joined the fray and they all started to burn merrily.

The path that the leaves and the sticks made pointed straight at the cabin. There was an unencumbered route that way, leaves and sticks and leftover newspaper... all of them began to smolder in preparation for being part of the conflagration. The little ember winked out, its work happily done, the fire was building, growing stronger, and heading towards the cabin.

From within the cabin there was a creak, a low moan as of someone who has drank too much and is choosing between the inevitable aching of his head or the clarion call of his bladder. The creaking grew louder, footfalls and then front door burst open. Without a glance, without even really being awake, the stream began instantly. The leaves felt it first, sputtering and then going out. The newspaper was next, soaked it could no longer burn. The little stick sizzled, and then finally the bigger stick sighed as it too was extinguished. The creaking went back the other way; the last ember of the fire glowed in the cold night air, and finally went out as well.

The End

Rains on the Deluvian Plains

A story of misdirection and guile by Dan Marvin

Riotous social discord followed the prince wherever he trod. It was, seemingly, an attribute which he alone possessed. If ever one were to want an insurgence on short notice, the prince could deliver. The only problem faced by the prince was that this was a difficult service to market as there was rarely a need for such a thing. In order to alleviate this strange aura, the prince set out on a journey to find Balatorm the Wise, wisest man in these, the three kingdoms of Gorg.

After three years of searching (strewing riotous social discord wherever he trod) the prince was at the end of his means and his rope. Various rumors had reached his ears over these intervening years and all they had done was lead him back basically to where he started. The only place in all of the kingdoms which had escaped his scrutiny was his own town, the city-state of Otimbe. He asked around.

He came to the shop of an old shopkeeper ('a good thing for a shopkeeper to keep' thought the prince) and looked at the window. "Maps for those seeking Balatorm the Wise- 14 sheckles" read the sign. The prince went inside. He inquired of the shopkeeper "where keepest thou the maps of which the window spaketh?" In a dry, foreign dialect, the shopkeeper intoned "soldest out are we of the maps to Balatorm. Perhaps triest ye next week and a shipment then may have in come." The prince pulled his rapier from where it was kept and smote the shopkeeper head and chest (in proper biblical fashion) and, in a fit of pique, he left.

Suddenly, from the street outside, the shopkeeper heard in his dying moments, the sounds of riotous discord. By the windows, the prince ran once more, doused with tar and covered with feathers. The shop keeper smiled and relaxed. The prince had found Balatorm.

The End

Phractured Philosophy – Without a doubt, the surest sign of aging is the realization that we need help to set the time on the new TV.

The Age of Innocence

Fiction from a different phylum by Dan Marvin

Staring back at them from the inside of the old box was the head of a badger, mounted in a menacing pose with beady glass eyes staring back at them, its jaw full of badger teeth snarling in a permanent grimace. The boy and the girl were startled at first, and then dissolved into peals of laughter when they realized the mammalian threat was largely ornamental. They continued pawing through Grandpa Joe's belongings in the attic, each discovery a realization that the man wasn't exactly right.

The uniform from the war had a few holes but the decorations still clung proudly to the faded cloth. A picture of him wearing this uniform in younger years left no doubt that he had been an attractive man with a firm, egalitarian chin and straightforward gaze. His eyes had dimmed somewhat over the years but when the chin set firmly, there was no way you were going to talk him out of what he had decided to do.

Towards the bottom was an unmarked box covered with years of dust, tied with a ribbon and unadorned with markings. Susie and Mark picked it up and looked at it in the dying light of a midwinter afternoon sunshine, slanting in through the vents. It held no clue as to what lay within. With a pull, the ribbon started to untie and then broke, disintegrating after years of lying undisturbed.

Inside was a stack of letters. They were addressed to Miss Josephine Marks and had been returned to Joseph Cullins undelivered. None had been opened, but they sat there begging the children to peek inside. At the bottom there was one, opened letter. This one was addressed to "My Darling Joe" and was written in the careful script of a lady of some refinement. Carefully, not wanting to rip the letter, they opened it.

"My Darling Joe" it repeated. "You know that I have always loved you, since the day we first laid eyes on each other in the five and dime. Your letters have brought me much happiness during a cold time in our nation's history. I'm not sure how to say this so I'll just say it... Papa says we have to move. He won't or can't tell me where just yet, but he says we must. I can't disobey Papa, especially not with you way over in Europe. I don't know when I'll write again, or from where, but I promise I will. Love always, Josephine."

The children looked at each other and then at the pile of unopened mail that had rested on top of this letter. They had all been sent to the address this letter was from, none of them had been opened. Obviously she had never written Grandpa Joe back. His devotion to her was stunning, even to a 12 and 10 year old. They didn't say a word as the closed up his trunk, putting everything carefully back from where it had come. Slowly they descended the stairs and walked to Grandpa Joe's room. He looked back at them from the chair, smiling. "Did you find any treasures?" He asked the children. Grandpa Joe," Mark started reluctantly, "Who was Josephine Marks?" As soon as the question was out of his mouth he wished he hadn't asked it. Grandpa Joe sputtered a moment and then smiled.

"She was a woman from in a magazine. Soldiers would write to her and she'd write back. After awhile, the government must have shut 'er down. You kids... you didn't read any of the letters I wrote to her did ya?" Was his reply. The kids shook their heads and Joe breathed easier. "Well, be off with ya now, and let me know when dinner is!" The kids scampered off and Grandpa Joe thought about Josephine Marks for the first time in 50 years. A tear formed in his eye.

The End

Questionable Quotation – "Neither a borrower nor a lender be. But if you have to pick one, be the borrower."

-Shaekspeare

Graphic Violence

Unadulterated happy-talk by Dan Marvin

Many years ago, there lived a woodsman named Francis. He spent his days chopping trees and turning them into logs to be used to build homes. His own home was a quaint cottage tucked into the trees on a little used road in the hamlet of Smythton.

Every day, he would get up, have his breakfast, kiss his wife, and go off into the countryside with his mule and a large saw. In the evening, he would return, tired but satisfied with his day's efforts. Weekly, he would hitch up the wagon and head into town, to trade his logs for food and other necessities at the center market. It was a simple life but a good one.

On the other side of Smythtown, lived a shrewish old man named Nikus with ice for a heart. He built shacks for people to live in and they paid him handsomely for the privilege. Every day, he would get up, count his money, kiss his reflection, and retire to his desk to dream up plots for making more money. Once a week, he would go to town to help pick out logs for his shacks at the center market.

After dinner on one particular Saturday, Nikus went to market earlier than usual. As it happened, he ran into Francis who had just arrived to sell his logs to the market manager. Nikus immediately had an idea. "Hello, kind woodsman," he said with as close to a smile as he ever got, "My name is Nikus. Instead of selling your logs to the market manager, and then having him sell them to me, what if we cut out the middleman and I bought them directly?"

This made sense to Francis who didn't have much of a head for business. "OK, let's try it and see what happens!" They haggled on a mutually beneficial price, Francis gave him the logs, and both went away happy.

The End

Author's Note - This story is in response to a number of suggestions that my stories are morbid, depressing, or just "downers." As you can plainly see, this story is rated G, has a moral (capitalism works) and is largely inoffensive. Of course, it's boring as dirt. Let me know if this is the sort of story you would like to see from now on.

Inspired by Fate

Small Insignificant Words Strung Together Thoughtfully by Dan Marvin

Many times, the sun had risen and set since the tribal elders had convened and cast Rising Wind adrift. His crime had been theft, his punishment lenient by Seneca standards, and his fate was sealed. With a tribe for support, a man could live 40 summers. Alone, he was lucky to survive half that. The bones had been rolled, luck no longer smiled upon him.

Still, a man had to live as long as he could. To the South he had heard of a clan that welcomed warriors, regardless of their crime. He must find that clan before the snows once more swirled. Many days of running had brought him to a land he had never before seen, the mountains had turned into plains and the valleys were replaced with ravines. It was a land of much water, game was plentiful, and eyes watched him wherever he went.

With the knowledge of his forefathers situated in his genes, Rising Wind found food among the strange foliage. When he was tired, he slept. The rest of the time, he looked for the clan. His cunning brought him through danger to the banks of a river the likes of which he had heard only in the stories of the elders by the fires of winter. He followed it for days, and finally he found the encampment.

Rising Wind was allowed to enter freely. He knew that he had passed many guards but he was unchallenged. In the center of the village, he shouted his name and held aloft an animal pelt he brought as a greeting. In time, an old man hobbled out of a shelter and looked him over. Through sign language and a few common words, they spoke.

Rising Wind told him of his long journey, skimping on details only in the reason for his trek. He told of the land of mountains and streams he called home, of the corn and squash they ate. He asked about this wonderful place where an outcast could find refuge. The old man beckoned for him to follow as he headed to his shelter.

There, the man took his pelt and gave him a box filled with cleaning supplies, inspirational tapes, and vitamin supplements. The next days were filled with sales tips, corporate visions, and, most of all, the idea that these were his true friends, he needed no others. Finally, he was sent back to the village of his elders to sell the wares. Rising Wind was the newest member of the Amway clan.

The End

Good, the Bad, and the Moves

Contemporary fiction by Dan Marvin

A bullet thudded hollowly on the side of a long vacant building. From its staring eyes, I followed the length of my assault weapon, knowing I would never find the lone sniper holding my troop at bay. The only chance I had was to run for it, launch a grenade and hope like hell I didn't get hit.

"Cover me, David!" I yelled with a tone to my voice that even I didn't recognize. It was a long ways from Dubuque, I thought as I lurched out of the back door and worked around to the street. Was it only 6 months ago that I had said goodbye to my folks and headed to basic training? Turns out, it had been a bad move.

You could have told me it was a lifetime and I'd have believed it, it sure seemed like another world to me. I thought about high school as I bellied down in a ditch to try to remain covered. A bullet coughed dust just ahead of me and some got in my eye. Not wearing my goggles had been a bad move.

Delores was quite a looker, back in my senior year! Her letter telling me that she was marrying Bobby Joe Hardaway came as quite a surprise, especially after I had spent everything I had made in 5 months on an engagement ring and had Bobby Joe give it to her. Bad move.

Compounding my heartache was the misfortune that had overtaken my family. Dad was gored by a bull, the first rodeo clown to die that way in Texas. Jumping out of the barrel was a bad move. My brother Roy fell off a cliff he was excavating for the government, just turned and fell right off the scaffolding! Bad move.

Mom's run in with the law had made all the papers. Holding up a police station turned out to be a bad move. All these thoughts raced through my mind as I stood up in the middle of the street. Turns out, it was a bad move...

The End

The President's Wife

A tell-all novel in 7 exciting paragraphs

In the early 2050's, I was lucky enough to be a trusted confidant of the president's wife. When she wasn't sleeping around or smoking crack, we would often sit on the verandah of the White House and throw water balloons at the secret service men below. Silly sods that they were they had to stand there and take it! No wonder one of them eventually killed her.

I remember my first discussion with her highness, it was just after the inaugural ball and she was tanked. I held her head high above the toilet as she released hors d'oeuvres back to water from which they came. Later, as she drank water and smoke unfiltered Camels, she began to tell me about her life. When she was growing up the Congressman (her father) was rather strict. He insisted on sending her to an all girl's school to keep her pure. Luckily, his guilt for missing her formative years also gave her an allowance sufficiently high that she could employ the groundskeepers to come up occasionally and get it on. The money also paid for beer and weed, with the leftover funds endowing a chair for the University and a degree for her.

Out in the world, she abruptly shacked up with a lawyer with much more ambition than brains. Together, they quickly scaled the ladder of politics until they were poised on the brink of the big one, the Presidency. Her father and her husband sometimes had to dispose of a contractor, gardener, or personal trainer when the blackmail got too expensive but this stage in her life was relatively tame.

When the election came, it was no surprise that her man won. She had groomed him well and his performance was outstanding. The flights around the world, huge parties, and illicit kickbacks were just starting and the first lady was delighted. Finally, here was a life worthy of her talents!

It all started to fall apart when the cocky young comedian came to play the White House on New Year's Eve. She was indiscreet when she invited him for a house tour and he seemed well educated in her lustful ways. The next day, his threats were real, his case was strong, and his stature was sufficiently high that he could not be eliminated.

When the photos began to appear in a popular men's magazine amid allegations of infidelity, she really hit bottom. It seemed like no amounts of pills and booze could fill the bottomless pit of her despair. It came almost as a relief when she asked me to help her end it all. With just the right amount of coercion, the secret service man was all too happy to snap and kill her. And now I am first lady.

The End

The Importance of Being at the Top of the Food Chain

A Biblical supplement by Dan Marvin

In the stultifying heat of the attic, the newspaper clippings divulged their news to no one in particular. A dress dummy sat waiting for a dress that would never be made. Toys from forgotten childhoods sat in abandon, pushed aside to make way for more. A yard sale would be a happy event for this collection of flotsam. Still, it lay in wait, ready to be important once more.

It was Lemond's first day out of the nest. He had been born into this world as the first of seven brothers. His mother had gotten hungry and eaten four of his siblings before he really got to know them well so he was now the oldest of three. The famished look in his mother's eyes told Lemond that it was time to leave.

He packed up his belongings, a set of functional whiskers, a long tail, and some paws for cleaning and headed on his way.

Luckily, since his brain was the size of a pea, he was blessed with instincts that told him how to behave. If it wasn't for generations of genetic codes that went before him on trial and error, Lemond would quite likely have been dead by now. Not that it was ever very far away.

First stop, food. He went into a convenient hole and emerged in a large room containing... food. He was happy. He ate heartily of old grease, some crumbs, and a bit of water splashed next to the sink. He avoided an irate woman with a large broom thing and scampered upstairs again.

Next up, a mate. He looked around, squeaked a bit, and soon had one. Where would they live? Lemond wondered, in a non-intellectual way. He looked around him and saw what was at hand. Hmmmm... newspapers, a roller skate, and a dress dummy full of stuffing. This stuff was great! He set about building a house for his new paramour.

They lived happily in the skate for many months. Their first litter was born in spring, and they raised them with a certain casual disregard until one day they were gone. He looked at his wife curiously when she burped after he asked where the kids had gotten off to.

A head appeared in the attic. It was followed by shoulders and a torso. Good lord! What was this? The hands picked up the roller skate, Lemond and all, and threw it into a bag. The eyes looked at the chewed newspaper, the fouled dress dummy, and clucked to itself in disapproval. Today was the day they would get rid of this junk.

The End

Two Sides to the Coin

Whisperings in the wind by Dan Marvin

She was a scholarly, bookish type, unaccustomed to the world of humans but possessed of a certain unintentional beauty. Her days were spent with her friends, the books, and her nights were filled with the rigors of cat ownership. Her simple world had a definite beginning and middle. The only thing that filled her with dread was the ending.

He was a loutish but beautiful brute, given to days-long binges and his path was strewn with the debris of dozens of failed relationships. His heart was hard, but inside was the one thought that made him cringe... was he unlovable? Could he ever love another? (OK, fine, so that's two questions but they are similar so I assigned them the same category -auth)

They came together one October night, she was coming out of the book shop where she sipped exotic blends of coffee and he was coming out of the bar where he gulped domestic brands of beer. The collision had the subtlety of a train wreck and the reaction was immediate and intense. He helped with her book, looked into her eyes, and felt a stirring in his soul the likes of which he thought happened only in the movies.

This huge stranger with the beer on his breath frightened her. Not because he looked mean, but because he was so CLOSE. She held her breath and let out a barely audible "thank you" when he helped with her books. Her mind raced as he offered a bit too hurriedly, to walk her home. She tried to say no, tried to turn and run, but instead nodded shallowly and showed him the way.

In a bit of bravado, she asked the man upstairs. Even more shocking, he accepted. They spent the night, not wrapped in emotional embraces but talking, going over their lives, bringing each other up to speed. He seemed fascinated by her mind; she was amazed by his body. When he left the next morning, they exchanged the briefest of kisses.

The days turned to weeks, the fall turned to winter, and love blossomed for the two mismatched soul mates. They found similarities in the strangest places, and their differences made their feelings all the more intense. He was gifted at dealing with the world; she was comfortable taking on an idea. Together, they made one whole person, and the spring time wedding was well attended.

The End

'So what the hell is this', you may be asking if you're a regular viewer. 'It has a happy ending, it's not funny, and it borders on well written. What gives, Dano?' Just suck it up and deal with it, hapless customer and when you write your book you can do it however you want.

Don't try this at home

Tales of the darkness that lies within us all by Dan Marvin

The empty beer bottles, burned out candles and pizza boxes somewhat obscured his form but Fenton was here, somewhere. His friends called him "loser" a somewhat optimistic opinion of his fortunes coined by someone he had long since alienated by not repaying debts or hitting or some such.

Two days after his spree began, he slowly emerged from his cocoon of rumpled bedding, reeking and in great pain. He stumbled to the bathroom and, had he had anything to bring up, would have vomited. Instead, he settled for soaking his head with tepid water from the tap and rinsing out his mouth with toothpaste and his finger.

Looking at his distorted image in the mirror Loser wondered if it was the glass that had somehow warped or if his retinas were responsible for the damage. Either way, it didn't help much. Sticky yellow material had filled in his eyes while he slept to spare him the sight. Undaunted by the crust, he forced himself to take a good look.

8 years earlier, Fenton had been on a very successful track. In pre-law, the son of immigrants was well liked by his peers and well regarded by his professors. He managed to maintain a B+ average and got by with part time work at an on-campus diner. That summer, his "friends" had turned him on to the force that would ultimately propel him to his private hell.

He had been using for 8 years. The money had dried up, the opportunity vanished, and his parents long since disowned him. His body was beginning to rebel at the long hours and constant punishment. His skin, beneath its healthy patina of dirt, was a pasty white. His hair was matted, his eyes red. He had begun to steal to support his habit.

With a crazed look, he sat down at the table once more and reached for a fix. His finger found the switch, the CPU booted up, his pace quickened. In a few minutes it was over. "Loser" had logged on.

The End

Questionable Quote – 'Spare the Rod and spoil the child." As quoted by my mother, when talking about her husband, Rod.

Life with Charley.

The altimeter continued its deadly descent; Flight 1366 was going down somewhere over Duluth. The Captain struggled valiantly with the controls but he had no power to convince the plane to head skyward once more. His frantic hands found the microphone and he warned the Flight Control tower to anticipate the worst.

The man in 2A was robust, loud, and very sweaty. Just about now he was wishing he was anywhere but here. The seminar he had just given in Kansas City would be his last. Deep inside, he was glad.

A woman in 12F slept fitfully, unaware of the unrest around her. Still, she was dreaming of falling, falling...

The young boy across the aisle held onto his armrests with all of his might. He had been very brave to say good-bye to his father, very brave to fly alone, back home to his mother, but he was not very brave at the moment. He was a very very scared little boy.

A stewardess stopped briefly and asked him to buckle up. Still trying to do her job, she was attempting to keep some semblance of order. The 14 degree list to port was not helping at all. The old line that items may shift during the flight stuck in her mind for some reason.

The farmer and his wife could hear a growing roar. They had just finished a late dinner and were settling in to listen to the television. It was not unusual to hear a distant airplane flying overhead. It was somewhat more unusual to hear one at 8000 feet and heading towards the front door.

Row 35, seat B was empty. The man sitting next to it was just as happy as he was using it as a table as he re enjoyed his lunch into an airsick bag. Waiting at home was his wife, his son, his life. Waiting in seat 35B was his brief future.

One hundred and twelve other stories filtered through one hundred and eight other heads. The schizophrenic in seat 22E reassured himself and himself under his breath. He thanked himself but suggested that there may be cause for alarm.

The remorseless altimeter continued its plunge, 4000, 3500, 3000... it was painful to watch and impossible not to. For the one millionth time, the captain tried to reignite the engines. Number 1 took and began to provide him with some power to fight back. At 300 feet, they reached the bottom of the parabola and began to head upwards once more.

As the farmer and his wife looked on, the plane continued to head for the house. They saw the faces of the passengers and the underbelly of the plane as it roared over the house and on to its emergency landing somewhere.

"Damn kids and their infernal machines" the farmer remarked and went inside.

The End

The Upright Path

Three lessons for a happier life by Dan Marvin

At wit's end, Cedric ran through the orchard. His aching feet would take him very little farther; the dogs behind him would soon be there. With a look of panic, he flopped beneath an apple tree for what would surely be his final respite. As he listened for the ever approaching canines, he absently began reading the graffiti scrawled on the side of the ancient apple.

"A wish for a thing will sure be granted, a wish for a feeling must always be denied" Cedric wondered who would have taken the time to write such a cryptic note on the side of an apple tree. It looked fresh but also was grown into the very heart of the wood.

"Wishes... I could use one right about now. I wish those dogs weren't after me!" Cedric muttered under his breath. A scurrying in the brush brought a family of rabbits into view. "Fine wishing tree this is, I ask for less animals, it gives me more."

Miraculously, however, the rabbits scurried off and soon after, the rising din that had been the dogs began to recede. There were chasing the rabbits! Cedric gazed up at the unthinking branches and his mind began to whirl. "I wish to be rich!" A bag containing one spark plug appeared. "I wish to be famous!" An accordion dropped from the branches. "Damn sarcastic trees" thought Cedric as he scooped up his assortment of useless tidbits and headed for town.

As he wandered up the road, he noticed a Rolls Royce with an elderly gentleman of obvious means looking beneath the hood. "Beg Pardon, guv'ner, what seems the problem?" Cedric asked.

The man looked his way and said "I've a dead spark plug. You don't have one about you, perhaps?" Cedric produced the bag, the spark plug fit, and the overjoyed gentleman paid him handsomely for it, as well as offering him a lift to town.

"You know how to play that thing?" The man asked, pointing at the accordion. "Sure don't" replied Cedric. "No matter, we need musical men like you at the new Polka club I'm starting. If you need a job, look me up!" With that, the man handed him a card.

Years later, Cedric the Accordion Man pulled his Lamborghini to a stop in front of the orchard. He got out and looked for the tree, his tree. He read the inscription once more and hoped his wish was possible. "You have given so much, wishing tree, but I am lonely. I want some warmth in me life."

With that, the tree gave a groan and toppled to the ground. "Rats, that's one wish I guess it just couldn't do. Shame to let this good apple wood go to waste, though." Cedric returned and cut up the tree for firewood.

The End

Don't Tell Don't Ask

Future fast forward by Dan Marvin

Pope Bob Pius IV sat on his holy can, doing his divine duty, and chuckling at the naughty antics of Trixie in the Sunday Hi and Lois comic strip. What a spunky toddler, he thought to himself as he wiped himself with papal TP. He tucked his remaining hairs into his very tall shower cap and cleansed his body all the while trying to think of relevant bible passages dealing with showering. He didn't suppose they showered much in Jesus' day, there weren't any passages he could think of dealing with it. It was his usual morning routine, thinking about the bible's lack of references to showers as he took one.

As he wandered downstairs, he scratched his most holy but largely ornamental reproductive organ and yawned a bit. His yellowing t-shirt and boxer shorts were in sharp contrast to the several gold rings which ornamented each hand. He passed priceless reminders of by-gone glory on that long journey to the kitchen, he had seen them so often he was largely immune to their glittery patina.

He asked for his usual cup of coffee and a danish which was already prepared for him. He blessed the food and then ate it with gusto. After demolishing the danish, the pope lit up a smoke and settled in to watch Geraldo. It was how he kept in touch with the world's problems and, man, were there a bunch of them!

"Maria" he asked the maid "what do you think I should speak of at mass today?" He had always been bad at thinking up fresh topics. World peace and community of man were way overdone, in his opinion. Maria giggled, he knew that she would not answer. The pope sighed and began to write.

The bells signaling mass intoned their exhortation to come in, be seated, and listen to the pope's yearly message. The throngs spread around the massive cathedral proved that he still had the power to pack 'em in. Let's see, average donation of $10 a head, 200,000 in attendance, wow, he could retire off just this one gig! He chuckled at the thought of ever needing a material possession; the pope thing was pretty lucrative in its own right.

After what seemed like interminable babbling by lesser cardinals, the Pope approached the podium. In a doddering manner, he cleared his throat and looked out at the masses. He opened his mouth, then shut it again, then opened it, then ran from the stage weeping. He threw himself into the pope mobile and sped out of the parking lot, endangering pedestrians and killing livestock.

Later, in the Rome County jail, Pope Bob Pius IV looked forlornly out of the bars at the policemen beyond. Sure, they might have him now, but he would die first, and when they showed up, he would exact a terrible vengeance. The Pope's eyes lit up momentarily and he expired.

The End

What else is there?

Random musings by Dan Marvin

I bought a car, the other day. A minivan, really. It could be the official end of my childhood, the beginning of my extended midlife crisis, or a wonderful stage of life filled with the joys of family and hair loss. The jury is still out. I never thought cup holders and an integrated child safety seat would be the selling points on my first new vehicle.

The 90's seem like a hostile time to live. Is it just me or does everyone hate everything? Why are we so pissed off? Let me go on record as saying it can't be coincidence that the meanest era in recent history is also the one in which country music has gained wide-spread popularity. I'm convinced that it is the root of all evil. That's why I'm pissed, I don't know what your problem is.

Oh, I have another bone to pick with you, while we're here. If no one responded to people selling stuff on the phone, people would stop selling stuff on the phone. By buying that stuff, which you probably don't need, incidentally, you convince the people selling it that more people might want their stuff. Which I don't. So stop buying stuff over the phone, please.

Do TV sitcoms strike you as slightly unrealistic? Everyone seems to have quirky friends that pop in unannounced and provide scads of entertainment. It's rare that we see the main characters spend 15 minutes in the bathroom reading Newsweek and running to catch the phone with their underwear down. Of course, if we saw that on a regular basis, we would long for the quirky friends, so never mind.

I'm not hip because I've never roller bladed. It seems like something a hip person would do, to me. It also seems unlikely that I will ever try it. The image that returns to my mind over and over is how much difficulty I have walking sometimes. If I can't negotiate life with two largish flat areas keeping me upright, what chance do I have of keeping balanced on a number of free rolling balls?

Oh, one last item. You should really be doing something else, right now. The End (for now)

Authors Note: I wrote this in the 90's when I had a plan to be the next Andy Rooney. Unfortunately, he's still alive I'm pretty sure and I never wrote any more like it. I include is here because it proves what a well rounded writer I am and provides a snapshot into those glory days of yesteryear. Oh, I have now roller bladed but I still don't think I'm hip. My son assures me that hip isn't even a word any more.

Three symbols for the earth

Contemporary fiction from Dan Marvin

From the writings of T'Keesh - 'Hath no creature so much soul as the zourbule, nor so little brain. He is, to God, the perfect enforcer.'

The bellowous crash of lightning was followed with precious little silence, the mountain wanderers of the Cor'nash clan huddled together beneath their skins, waiting sleeplessly for the rare mountain storm to pass. For nearly 18 hours they had gathered thus, weathering the wrath of God and praying for his mercy.

It seemed as if mercy was far from the mind of God this night. The winds tore at their meager hovels and sleet was on the tongue of it. The cold was piercing. Something must be done. The clan looked to their leader.

D'bune gathered up his 4'7" and stood before them, a mighty pillar facing the winds. "Take me, oh Lord, spare thy children!" His normally strong voice was largely washed away in the swirling winds and the moans of the living rock. The clansmen watched anxiously to see what he would do.

With a terrifying look on his face, D'bune faced God with all of the purity he could muster and flung himself off of the precipice, sacrificing himself on the rocks below. The terrified Cor'nash looked at one another and then at the crag that had claimed their leader. The ominous clouds began to disperse.

"D'bune has won!" The cry was heard from mountain top to mountain top. The last of the food was made ready and the Cor'nash rejoiced, praising their leader and celebrating well into the night.

The next day they held the primaries to elect their next leader...

The End

80's flashback – Leg warmers were never a good fashion idea.

Along the way

Eurotrash fiction by Dan Marvin

The southbound road to Devlinshire wears history like a comfortable shawl. For centuries, the feet of conquerors, conquered, and the people caught in the middle have turned a 12 foot wide strip of countryside into a living history. Although you've probably heard the stories of the huge conquests, the wars, celebrations, and retreats, you probably have not heard the story of Lincoln McCleod and his 7 derbies or of Ronson O'Neil's misfortunes at the hands of some precocious grade school girls. No, these are the stories that time and distance erase, unless they are set down in print. Here is but one of those stories.

I sat in the pub, sipping an ale and checking my watch. I was fairly certain she had forgotten about our date, it was hours past the appointed time, but I really had nothing better to do. I had brought my sketch book and was biding my time putting down some thoughts before they left my head. A pretty horse stared out at me from a giant crater on some far off moon. On the next page, three nurses play bocce with Hitler. I didn't mean to suggest that they were good thoughts.

The door opened and in walked a stunning redhead. I was never much for the type; they always seemed a little too dangerous, like they could ruin my neat little world with a glance. This one possessed that look, but it was tempered with an expression of despair so deep that I felt my heart jump into my throat. I stumbled over my feet as I stood and asked if she needed help.

"Are you Dean Rothman?" she asked. The times that I had wished I was Dean Rothman in my lifetime were precious few, but this was one of them. "Indeed I am not good lady" was my response, my years of stodgy training paying off by keeping me from seeming in the least bit interested in her plight. That quickly faded as she burst into tears.

I offered her my handkerchief, but instead she grabbed onto me and held on for dear life. She cried until I didn't think her body could possibly produce more saline. I looked on, an ineffectual onlooker witnessing the coming apart of a stunning redhead. By and by, she quit the histrionics and looked me square in the eye. "You will help me find him?" it was more a statement than a question.

"No, I can't, I mustn't, well, of course" was my ingenious reply. I followed her out the door and we came round the corner of the pub. Dean was sitting there on his winded horse, looking a bit the worse for wear but clearly here.

He lifted the lady up behind him, tipped his hat, and rode off. Her eyes were locked on him, she never looked back at me or offered me thanks. Still, I felt that I had helped her, in some small way. I returned to the pub and downed 8 or 12 more pints of ale before my date arrived. But that is another story entirely....

The End

Spacesick

Riveting science fiction by Dan Marvin

The sickening 'thud' of the meteorite and the sound of metal splintering was the final testament to the 17 men and women of AirPod Delta, the research wing of the Lunar colony. The worst thing about the incident wasn't the horrifying conclusion, but the events that led up to it and immediately following.

From the Captains Log:

07:44:16 Science officer Jenson reports a large object nearing our position at a high rate of speed. Early spectrometric reports indicate an iron bearing meteorite of a size capable of instantly destroying any section of the colony it touches. I will solicit ideas for possible outcomes immediately.

09:13:07 It has been determined that the trajectory of the meteorite will indeed wipe out one section of the base, most likely the lab. Unfortunately, there is insufficient life support in the remaining sections to house all of the lunar personnel.

11:33:49 Current estimates are that we can sustain life support for 20 of 38 personnel from the lab area after meteorite impact until the next shuttle arrives in three months. The selection process has begun. First off are the people with the most useful skills and the younger workers who don't earn as much.

13:17:50 The selection process is complete, the 18 men and women who are to remain behind have been sedated and placed in the AirPod. All connections have been retracted, they are totally self sufficient. Lt. Decker has agreed to stay with them to make sure they stay sedated and in case the impact does not occur as predicted.

16:03:07 No contact with Lt. Decker, the assumption is that he wants to go out with dignity. Impact estimated in 12:02

16:15:10 AirPod D destroyed in meteorite collision. No life signs are determined, none were expected.

17:01:01 Must be in all the excitement, we forgot that all the bathrooms were in AirPod D. Estimate that at current rate of output, human excrement levels will become toxic in 97 days, 16 hours, 5 minutes. I will solicit ideas for possible outcomes immediately.

The End

Several Miles from Shore

A tale of warning by Dan Marvin

In the far off land of Hybernia lived a simple man with a non-taxing lifestyle. During the day, he busied himself with woodworking. At night, he relaxed by the fire with a snifter of brandy and a good book, immersing himself in the worlds created by hands other than his, living lives that he could not. On the weekends, he would trek to the nearby village to trade his handmade wares for food and more books. He was known as a scholarly nomad, capable of creating items of great beauty but somewhat devoid of it himself.

On one weekend excursion, a particularly striking woman happened by the marketplace, looking for a bookshelf that was 'just so' in her words. The man had no such bookshelf but offered to create it for her to her exact specifications. They settled on a time for her to come to his house to give him her vision for this piece of furniture. When the allotted hour arrived, he was sitting in his usual place, reading a book and sipping brandy when her knock jarred him from his reverie.

A quick look at his wrist confirmed his worst fears, something untoward was occurring. He choked down the sickening fear and opened the door to the interloper, greeting her with a smile and the invitation to a cup of coffee. Instead, she spied the brandy left on the hearth and inquired if she might have one of those. With his eyebrow cocked in amusement and interest, he poured the libation for her, knowing that brandy is a highly personal taste. One sip and she cooed "Oh yes, this is perfect. Thank you!" They puzzled over her rough sketch at the table for what seemed like hours until he glanced at his wrist once more.

"Goodness!" He exclaimed. "Has it really been five hours? I must sleep! And you must go, what will the villagers say?" Her look said all that needed to be said further and their lips locked in a passionate kiss, the tension that had been building all evening and only slightly alleviated by the brandy in their stomachs exploded into a kiss of such awe inspiring intensity that they both recoiled when it was done.

"Yes, I must go" She said, and was gone. She ran across the village gossip when she fled from his house but paid her no heed. The next day, the streets were filled with the word. The woman was scorned, her sewing business dried up and she was left penniless and destitute. The simple man became a hero to the townsfolk. Over the fire, his exploits were exaggerated in song and he took to believing them himself.

Years later, whenever a young buck would ask about womenfolk, he was always steered to the not so simple man sipping brandy by the fire in the Inn. There, he would hear about the night of passion in the woods.

The End

Like two ships...

Nautical nonsense by Dan Marvin

A far off wail was the signature of the SS *Darling of the Sea* and it was a mournful sound on a dark, foggy night. This far into the voyage, few would hear the sound. The *Darling* WAS mournful, it had been a long voyage and she was tired. There were days to go until they were at the sunlit shores of Tahiti, but even there, she would still be working, ferrying tourists to points of interest by night, waiting for their return by day.

As it happened, there was another soul to hear her cry this night. The HMS *Godfrey* was plying these waters as well, coming back filled with containers of tropical delights to sell to unwary consumers. He was older than *Darling* but still her whistle sent a shiver down his bow; he could tell that she was a beauty by the unwavering note of her signal.

Godfrey sent out his claxon blast, letting *Darling* know that they would pass close by. Soon, he heard her respond; there was excitement in her voice. Must be young and lonely, he thought as he answered once more. His pulse began to race and he picked up three knots in the turbid waters, his propeller surging with a youthful vigor that surprised him.

The two ships chatted back and forth for awhile, finding out that they had much in common but many differences too. She was young and energetic, he was more cautious but still enthused to talk to another ocean traveler. They passed by and agreed to talk again in a few weeks. It seemed to *Godfrey* that the time would never pass.

The next several months were filled with chance encounters; the two ships became very close indeed. *Godfrey* always showed restraint while *Darling* was impetuous and fun. Together, they made beautiful travel together. The seas were their playground and soon all the other ships were envious of how well they were getting along.

One day, as luck would have it, *Godfrey* received some shocking news. The trade had dropped off of late and he was being shipped out to more lucrative waters. He was aghast! Today was to begin his last journey where he would meet *Darling*. The freighter sailed off, but without the pleasure he usually had at the beginning of each voyage.

Sure enough, 4 days out they heard each other. He told *Darling* the bad news. For a long time she was silent. Then he shuttered when he heard the reply... 'We must be together.' Frantically he asked what she meant, told her it would be OK, but to no avail. When at last they emerged from the fog, they were on a collision course. The two ships collided in the open sea and sank slowly to the Ocean's bottom. *Darling's* keel lay across *Godfrey* and they were happy in perpetuity.

The End

On the Stationary Bike to Hell

Contemporary fiction by Dan Marvin

Judge Hawthorne looked down from between his brushy eyebrows and gave Randolph a look that would have frozen mercury. His lips twitched with disdain as he raised his gavel. "I find you in contempt of court, young man. Bailiff, please escort Mr. Hill down to the detainment cell." The relative gentleness of his demeanor belied the bile in his look. Randolph Hill was under no delusions, he would not be allowed out of the slammer until he divulged his information, under oath.

How had he gotten into this mess? He had never been an overly bright man. His teens had been spent raising hell with a group of kids looking for the back door to the top. Hard work and restraint were generally considered weaknesses. When he started dabbling in the fine art of sales and marketing of a product that was not exactly legal, his problems had begun in earnest.

He remembered the night vividly, Jimmy the Blade had been there, Two Toe Tommy arrived right on time. Words were exchanged and suddenly Two Toe Tommy was dead and Randolph Hill found himself with a knife to his throat. "If word of this gets out" Jimmy had snarled, "I'm going to turn you into Cheddar!" Although Jimmy's analogy was not quite up to snuff, Randolph was not likely to forget his point. He spent the rest of the week hiding at his brother's apartment until the police arrived to haul him off to jail. If he didn't talk, he was a goner. If he did talk, he was a goner. Randolph Hill decided that sometimes life was not fair. The cot creaked beneath his not insignificant weight and he studied his new home. It measured a roomy 10x12 feet, they had spared no expense. The toilet was stainless steel and the mirror above the sink was not glass. He stretched out to think. Hours later, a bailiff came to see him. "You ready to talk?" the bailiff asked gruffly. Randolph stood and walked to the bars.

"Yes" he replied with resignation. He climbed the stairs to the courtroom and resumed his place in the witness stand. "Mr. Hill, you are still under oath. The question before you is 'What restaurant makes the best Ziti in Chicago?'" the judge asked for the 100th time.

"Mama Mioni's" Randolph said quietly. A man stood up in the courtroom and fired a single shot into Randolph's skull. In the confusion, he blended into the crowd outside and was gone.

Downtown, Mama Mioni prepared for the worst.

The End

Fascist Florists

A story of oppressive romance by Dan Marvin

It was a bleak, heavenly day, just right for light hearted banter about death, dying, and the upcoming fair. Rock Spaz sat on the cold comfortable bench and dejectedly considered how much fun the fair would be. The morbid clowns, listless performing seals, and the excited wails of children danced in his sad eyes.

Rock loved the circus and hated it. The wretched smells of cooking popcorn, the pleasure of midway hucksters taking his hard earned cash, the wonderful cacophony of the tinny music of overpriced rides were all pleasures that left him spent and weak. He could hardly contain himself for another horrible, wonderful week.

Rock stood up and surveyed the bleak landscape before him, the cheery clouds floating by in the eerie sunlit sky; the horrible laughter of children playing in the fetid park, all of these greeted his eyes as he moaned with joy. "Hey Spaz!" a lighthearted voice of doom greeted him. He knew that frightening voice that lifted his spirits with every word.

"Mary!" He shouted softly. "Mary Poffinmiler! I haven't seen you in ages! Did you get that root canal you were telling me about yesterday?"

"Yes" was the worried but enthusiastic reply. "It was terrific! If you get a chance to see a dentist, make sure he's free with the pliers!" Mary turned on her heel quickly and limped away with agony and a spring in her step. Rock stood by as he rushed forward to keep up with her.

"That made no sense!" He said with no trace of question in his voice. "Did he pull some teeth?" The query died on his lips as he practically yelled at her.

Instead of answering, Mary replied. "No, but I wish he had!" She then fell into a manhole. His deaf ear heard her lament "Hooray! I fell into a manhole! "Rock wandered about aimlessly with a sense of purpose. Later he slept fitfully like a log and awoke with a gnawing pain in his gut. "God no!" he said happily. "The contradictions are wreaking havoc with my system!" With a smile on his face, he died. Rock and Mary lived happily ever after.

The End

The Beginning

God's best friend

Contemporary fiction by Dan Marvin

More quickly now, Norman heard the buzzing 'fzzzt' and heard the plaintive yelp after each. The dogs were testing the defenses, becoming more bold and brazen in their attack. How had they gotten so intelligent? He was supposed to study them, but now he was the one under the microscope. He and his untested defense system that was seeing its first real life application.

The rogue dogs of the deep Brazilian jungle had become a bit of a myth in the last few years. Stories would occasionally filter back to civilization of towns wiped out, the citizens strewn far over the countryside, victims of the devil dogs. Herds of cattle would vanish, their bodies never found. Logging crews resorted to sleeping in their vehicles and even then would be killed when nature called. The deep jungle was quickly becoming a place that no one would visit. No one, that is, except Norman Peel.

Norman's specialty was debunking modern myths. He had gathered information vital to controlling killer bees and had set up residence in ant hills. He had slept with wild bears and lived to tell. He wasn't brave as much as he was prepared, his methodical testing, building, and retesting made his expeditions safe and sane. All except this one.

The night before last, he had the first contact with the mongrels. At dusk he saw skulking shadows in the trees and the next morning found foot tracks in his campsite. A bag of food had been ripped open but otherwise nothing had been disturbed. Looking back on it, he was sure they were just sizing up his defenses somehow. The next night he could see their shining eyes in the glow of the campfire as the red beams held them at bay. In the morning, he found the remains of several animals he hoped were deer piled on the perimeter.

Tonight, the attack had begun silently. At dusk he wondered if they had continued moving onward. Now he knew better. The soft 'pop' of perimeter mines was interspersed with the sound of the energy beacons being tripped. He was sure that there were no casualties on their side and only hoped that there were none on his. So far the fence had held. So far technology was winning. It was a long night. Twice dogs had broken through somehow and had to be sent away with the dart gun. He got a chance to examine one that had been sedated and was amazed at how intelligent its eyes were, seeming to question him even as they sized him up for dinner. "I just want to study you pooch" he answered the silent question.

Finally, dawn broke and so did the attack. The dogs trotted one by one into the jungle and the motion sensors quieted. Birds began to sing and Norman stood his weary being up. He felt his snout beginning to grow and his canine teeth were definitely longer. Norman started to worry.

The End

If it seems like a good idea, sometimes it is and sometimes it isn't.

Words of wisdom from Dan Marvin

The well shaft had an almost otherworldly glow about it as Nicorus looked down. He knew intellectually that there could be no glow there; the shaft was as black as the night. Still, the longer he stared, the more real became the shifting patterns he saw beneath him. He felt compelled by invisible hands to join the lights. With hardly a thought, Nicorus climbed over the side and jumped.

At first, he wasn't sure where he was. Or who he was. Or why he was. Slowly, as the throbbing of his cranium began to ebb, he sensed dampness around him. Above, very far above, he saw an off center circle that was somewhat brighter than the gloom surrounding it. Above that, there seemed to be stars. His hands came up in front of his face, he knew they were there, but he could not see them. What had happened to his glow?

The rough edges of the walls let him know immediately that the well had been haphazardly dug and probably was not altogether a safe place to be. Still, he figured that he would die of starvation long before the shaft collapsed so he should consider himself lucky. At this thought, a wry smile crept to his lips and calmed him some. He began to search more earnestly.

To his right, the wall jutted away and he haltingly followed it. Although he couldn't tell, there seemed to be a tunnel jutting away from the main shaft. He crept forward, careful to test each step for a solid floor. Sure enough, the small circle of starlight above suddenly winked out. Nicorus began to feel a stirring of excitement. He HAD been right; there was something here, something interesting! Each footfall took him farther from life as he knew it.

In the distance now, there was light, actual light, growing a bit stronger with each step. It seemed like the tunnel went on forever and he was working on 28 hours with no sleep. Still, the gentle glow soon illuminated the slimy walls of the tunnel he was in and showed him where to step to avoid the rocks and hollows below his feet. Finally, the light source showed itself, a crevice in the wall in front of him.

Nicorus put his eye to the crack in the wall and peered through. He quickly stumbled backwards when he realized there was another eye peering back at him! Summoning his courage further, he looked again. The eye was still there and he heard a voice. "Excuse me," came a refined and not unpleasant voice. "I'm stuck down a well! I've been here a frightfully long time, can you help me?"

The adventurous spirit went out of Nicorus like a flashlight being turned off. Without answering, he sat on the ground and put his head in his hands.

The End

Several Days Beyond Over

Contemporary fiction by Dan Marvin

Finished with his pasta, Eroni sat back from the table with a satisfied smirk. His heart raced at the exertion of eating and a thin bead of sweat glistened on his forehead. The glow of hunger satisfied soon became the anticipation of dessert unsampled. When the waitress reappeared, she was sent back with an order for Death by Chocolate and a black coffee.

Minutes later, with Death by Chocolate suitably devoured and no way to avoid the inevitable any longer, Eroni signed his name on the dotted line and pushed his way up from the table. More correctly, he pushed the table away from himself to get enough room to stand. He swayed briefly and lurched towards the men's room, the need to get rid of coffee and beer overcoming his usual unwillingness to move.

His zipper back in its up position, Eroni began the long, ponderous way to the front door. As usual, Amil wished him well and told him to come back often. Secretly, Eroni wondered if he would be so cordially dismissed if he did not single handedly keep the Little Italy restaurant in the black. He didn't consider it for too long, not wanting to admit that he was largely dislikable. Or large and dislikable.

Eroni waddled to his car which creaked miserably beneath his weight. The broken shocks had long ago given up on the possibility of protecting him from the bumps of the road beneath. He swung his way onto Mansini and turned left on 37th. Tonight, instead of heading straight home, he was possessed to drive a bit further. Oak and Briquette passed by, as did Harmony and Suede. He reveled in the relative mobility his Toyota afforded him. Just by providing it gas, it gave him so much. It may have been the beer talking.

Ten minutes later, it was definitely the beer talking as the officer pulled the belligerent Eroni from the comparatively minuscule car and began to read him his rights. Belatedly, officer Carone realized that the back door of his vehicle would never hold this behemoth. With a disgusted look, the officer dismissed him and helped him back into his car. His bulk was good for something, after all.

Eroni turned around and drove slowly home. Even though he was off the hook, the officer had been right. He had been driving erratically and that was dumb. A rarely chastened Eroni opened the door to his house and sat in his favorite chair. He was still there, hours later, when the police knocked on the door and broke in. They wanted to ask him questions about his very thin neighbor who had been found dead of a heart attack on the sidewalk in front of his house. Eroni apologized for not hearing the door and smiled inwardly as he described the health nut who had been his neighbor.

The End

West Side Morning Glory

Contemporary fiction by Dan Marvin

In the squalid decay of inner city rot, a single flower bloomed in a field strewn with refuse. It had aimlessly drifted here as a pollinated seed weeks earlier, wafting this way and that, held aloft by a column of turgid city air. The seed had fallen, screaming softly, into a pile of dog excrement.

For the longest time, Buttercup had laid dormant, held within the seed by the doubt of what she would find on the outside. It had looked foreboding and uninviting, not the kind of place a self respecting young flower should be on a nice spring morning. Still, she had a yen to see what life was about and spread her petals to the smog obscured sun before she packed it in and called it quits. With resolute timidity, Buttercup slowly began putting down roots.

The dog waste was the perfect bed for her; she grew rapidly as the slightly acidic rain beat down from above.

It was chilly at first, but after a few days the weather broke warm and inviting and Buttercup was glad she had chosen to set up shop after all. In a few days, the hard part was over and she opened her petals to the day for the first time. From afar, she could have been a scrap of paper, a shard of cloth. Still, somehow, she managed to be distinct and beautiful.

As she was growing, she noticed other seeds floating above, not looking down at the barren landscape at all. After her petals unfolded, she began to notice that other seeds were landing nearby. Within a few days, she had company, other wildflowers, drawn by her determination and pioneer spirit. She greeted each as they emerged from the ground and encouraged them to sprout and grow.

Slowly, the abandoned lot was beginning to take on a new appearance. Buttercup spun off a few siblings of her own and noticed the first bees had found their way to her field. That was she thought of it as now, her field. No longer an abandoned lot, choked with litter and ugly grass, it had become an island of beauty in a sea of despair.

One day, something new happened. A group of people showed up with brooms and rakes and garbage bags. The garbage was picked up, the old tires carted away; the empty hypodermic needles were carefully collected and disposed of as well. Buttercup's stamen swelled with pride as she surveyed her field. Her brothers and sisters and friends looked on with a similar sense of satisfaction when the people had left.

It was nearing the end of summer when Buttercup noticed the newcomer. He was scruffier than the rest of her friends and had a bad attitude when she tried to talk to him. She heard the whispers of 'dandelion' when people thought she wasn't listening. His buddies soon began popping up, bad characters like himself. Soon, they were picking on the other flowers and taking up all the nutrients. Slowly, the trash and debris began to drift back in. One by one, her friends began to die off from neglect.

Buttercup held on into the fall, but she knew the end was near. When it was time, she sent aloft a bevy of seeds, hundreds. They fell in line on the winds with the thousands of dandelion seeds. She watched them go, wishing them well and praying they too would find a nice bed of dog poop to land in.

The End

Erroneous Excerpt – "There it was again, a sodden thump from nearby sounding for all the world like a bag with a dead body being flung repeatedly to the floor. With my heart in my throat I rounded the corner and found an old woman beating a carpet that hung over the clothes line."

Steve King – "The Boring"

The Ignominy of Being Organic

Contemporary fiction by Dan Marvin

A straggling wisp of life force struck the denuded branch of a grape vine and stirred within. The force rested for a bit, it had been a long trip. The weather outside began to warm and with it, the life force strengthened. With a burst of energy, it sprung forth, first as leaves to gage the climate, and ultimately as a bunch of fine purple grapes, ripening happily in the sun.

When it was dry, they had water, when insects threatened, they were dusted. All in all, this was the good life. The day came, however, when the free ride must end. A sweaty, swarthy man came and plucked the bunch of life force and threw it rudely into a basket. The basket sat in the hot sun for an hour and was bundled onto a truck with no shock absorbers to be herded into a largish cave. Things looked bleak. Soon, they would get bleaker.

It was always unclear to the life force when he was supposed to leave. Sometimes, he headed out when someone looked the wrong way at him. Sometimes, he stuck around until his being had been as widely dispersed as he dared contemplate, rejoining at the last moment and looking for another barren place to start again. It made for an interesting life, all in all. In this case, he decided to ride it out to the bitter end. Given the choice later, he might have reconsidered.

First, he was thrown into a vat. Stamping feet separated him considerably, bits of him drifting to the far corners of the vat. Immediately, bacteria began altering his sugars into alcohol which kinda tickled. He chuckled as he became entombed in the oak barrel. He fermented merrily for awhile and started to get a little bored. The cask held him contained more solidly that he had anticipated so he had to wait it out. It HAD to get better than this! Months later, he was strained with parts of his skin ripped away and mostly his fluids traveling onward. We would have gotten out then but he was asleep. He only awoke as he began flowing again. He gathered what was left of himself and emptied into one bottle. There he sat, for years.

Movement! Thank God, there was movement! The cork twisted and then departed. With gusto, he shot out of the bottle and into a fat man's nose. There, he was sneezed out of existence. "Take this bottle back, it has no life" said the fat man.

The End

Two degrees of separation

Inspective fiction by Dan Marvin

Hiristocontenese was the ant king, favored drone of the Queen ant and king of the hill, so to speak. He spent his day in royal splendor, grooming the eggs and seldom venturing to the outside world. At a quiver of his mandibles he could have another ant dismembered for looking at him wrong. Since every time an ant looks at something he sees 288 pictures of it, looking wrong at someone is a huge slight. Hiristocontenese would not put up with it.

One fine summer day, Hiristocontenese was deeply absorbed in some reports from the aphid mines. The dew harvest was down this autumn and they would need the resources if they intended to weather what was shaping up to be a difficult winter. He shook his head and abdomen back and forth in disgust, he would have to touch antennae with Mirt, the brainless leader of the farming colony. As he was pondering the fates of the hill, his pheromone sensor began fluctuating wildly. The Queen needed him!

Hiristocontenese sprinted to the royal chamber as fast as his six legs would carry him. Once there, he kneeled respectfully before his highness and waited for her counsel. "Hiristocontenese," she started softly, "My days are numbered. I can feel the weakness of age wearing on my body. I know that our custom says the hill must pass with me but I feel it is time for us to break with tradition. You must create a new hill with a new Queen. Move my subjects there that life might continue even if mine does not."

There was no arguing with the Queen. Hiristocontenese sped away to begin arranging the move. His antennae quivered with orders to this worker and that, they prepared eggs for transport, gathered the food provisions, scouts went out to look for a new site. When the scouts returned, all was ready for the move. Workers were dispatched to begin the tunnels. Hiristocontenese went to the Queen's chambers to inform her that preparations were complete. She was dead.

Digging commenced immediately. Miles of tunnels were carefully crafted from the sandy soil. Special chambers were scattered strategically where they would stay warm in the winter but would be cooled by the summer breezes. The Queen would have been pleased.

Finally it was ready, the new hill had nooks for the eggs and the provisions had been moved. One special egg had the makings of a Queen and Hiristocontenese himself carried it up and over the lip of the hill. His antennae shook slightly as he scanned the surroundings, it was now or never. He gave the order to "march!" and off they went. 1/4 of the way, 1/2 way, 3/4, they were going to make it! A strange hum in the distance was the first sign that anything was wrong.

The hum grew louder and a huge contrivance dove into sight. "RETREAT!" Hiristocontenese commanded and the column quickly turned tail. The lawn mower hit the column halfway back to the old hill. Hiristocontenese felt himself flung threw the air, the egg he had been carrying fell to the ground with a disheartening 'pop.'   As he lay, broken and dazed on the grass, Hiristocontenese knew that he had failed his Queen. Overhead the owner of the lawnmower chuckled a little as his blades bit into the soft earth of the ant mound. "Better be careful," he thought, "wouldn't want to get stung."

The End

Phundamental Philosophy – Face it, we're fascinated with death and home invasions and accidents if for no other reason than to confirm that even if things are kind of crappy, at least we're better off than *that* guy.

Dear Reader.... In an attempt to further involve you in the story writing process, I have come up with a number of potential beginnings for my next story. Please look through the list and email me your favorite. In a perfect world, I would then take that information and act on it. This will determine if the world is, indeed, perfect.

A. The sweat was dripping from my brow, my fingers were raw and tingling, but the clarinet and I had reached an understanding.

B. From beneath the continental plates, the titans reared their heads once more, ready to reclaim the earth for the sleeping gods Bob had awakened.

C. From the far corners of the kingdom, serfs and nobles alike came to pay homage to the baby, none of them realizing the reign of terror he would bring upon them in 13 scant years.

D. Aglow with the inner peace that comes with understanding, I closed my eyes for the last time and drew my final breath.

E. Over the ridge was a cabin, and inside the cabin was the prettiest set of eyes a man was ever likely to see.

F. The blood trickled unnoticed down my cheek, I had solved the case but lost the woman, the sort of ending no private eye cares to contemplate.

G. The pulsating roar of the large jungle cats grew nearer now, I knew my water deprived legs would soon stumble and they would be upon me.

H. I stared at the screen in disbelief and waited for the cursor to move again on its own.

I. The raging torrents had sentenced the ship to death but our love had kept us together.

J. I knew that in five minutes, the indium tip on my watch would interact catastrophically with the ion deprived explosive pile buried deep inside the base of the building, but still I waited.

W. The doctors said I wasn't short enough to be a midget but damn it, I FELT short enough.

R. The cyclical patterns of abuse were well documented and understood but it was little consolation when they were aimed at you.

7. My boobs hurt which was disconcerting because, last time I had checked, I was a man.

Bogo's Revenge

A children's story by Dan Marvin

The forest was glistening with dew when Bogo poked his nose out of the small hole that was his home. He sniffed the pine scented air nervously. The Rascal brothers had been there, he could tell. It might have been last night or it might have been early this morning, but they had been there. Bogo did not like the Rascal brothers. They were mischievous raccoons who teased poor Bogo whenever he went looking for food. They would wait beside the path he was on and jump out at him when he was eating his seeds. They would take his straw he was using to build his nest and throw it into the wind, never to be seen again. Yes, they had been there and were probably waiting for him right now, plotting their next caper.

Most mornings, Bogo would scurry out of his hole and race up the path, trying to outrun them. Even though he was a speedy chipmunk, he was no match for the much longer legs of the raccoons. In no time they would be on him, laughing and stealing his food all morning until their mother called them to come for lunch. Only then could he snatch a quick meal. This morning though, Bogo sat in his hole and thought for a long time. How could he get the Rascal brothers to leave him alone?

After awhile, he saw shadows under the shrubs. He knew it was the raccoons, wondering where he was. Already by changing his routine he had made them nervous. Bogo wished he had a big dog for a friend. Raccoons didn't like dogs, and dogs didn't like raccoons, always it had been this way. But Bogo didn't have a dog for a friend, or any large animal that would make the Rascal brothers leave him alone. So he sat in his hole, thinking very hard, his whiskers twitching in the still early morning breeze.

Suddenly, Bogo smiled. He had a plan! It was a wonderful, marvelous plan. It had to work, it just had to! He scurried out of his hole and raced past the Rascal brothers. The race was on! Just as they did every morning, they chased Bogo, laughing and taunting him. "Run little chipmunk, run!" they yelled. And he did run.

This morning, instead of running towards his usual sunny spot where the seeds were plentiful, he headed off into the bushes. At first, the Rascal brothers followed him quickly, still laughing and yelling. Soon the bushes became pricker bushes, the little Bogo ran on ahead easily but the Rascal brothers began to slow. "Hey Bogo, there's no seeds in here!" they yelled.

Bogo finally came to a stop and sat panting under a large blackberry bush. He smiled to himself as he heard no signs of pursuit. Suddenly, Bogo heard a different kind of noise though. "Help help! Someone help us!" It sounded like the muffled voices of the Rascal brothers. Bogo thought they were playing a trick on him to get him to come out, but the noise went on for many minutes and showed no signs of getting any closer. If anything, the voices sounded more and more worried. Bogo sighed and started back along the path, following the voices.

He stopped under one of the bushes where the voices seemed the loudest. "Where are you?" He called out, still worried that he would be pounced at any moment.

"Down here!" came the voices, he looked around and finally made out a place where the grass was missing. Carefully he went to the edge of the hole and looked down, and there looking back were two sets of very worried eyes. "Bogo, you have to help us! We fell down in this hole and can't get out!"

Bogo considered it for a minute... if he walked away someone else would surely help the raccoons and they would have learned a lesson. Still, he couldn't leave them down there, a fox might come along and find them to be a tasty dinner. With his mind made up, Bogo looked around for something that might help.

Finally, in a tree above the briar patch he saw it. Quickly he scurried up the tree trunk and gave his mightiest push. "Look out!" he yelled as the branch fell, straight into the hole. In no time two frightened looking raccoons scurried up and out of the hole and stood blinking in the morning light.

"Bogo, you saved us!" He had never heard them sounding thankful before, he kind of liked it. He made his way down the tree trunk and cautiously approached the brothers. They both came up and gave him a high five. "You're a hero!" The raccoons put him on their shoulders and carried him to his favorite sunny place and spent the rest of the morning finding seeds for him.

For the rest of the summer, Bogo enjoyed the friendship of the Rascal brothers, they would come each morning and play with him until it was time for their lunch. And at last when the fall leaves fell and Bogo settled into his hole for the winter, he thought back to that one magical day when he'd had his revenge... not by getting even, but by doing the right thing. With a smile, he went to sleep.

The End

Authors Note – This story became a children's book when my daughter Cassie illustrated it for me. She did a very good job of bringing Bogo and the Rascal brothers to life. Look for it!

Three cushions for comfort

Contemporary fiction by Dan Marvin

Five stories up, from the ledge in front of the window to Archer, Anderson, and Peabody, CPA Claddius sat, perched precariously viewing the scene below. The beeping of taxis and the mad rush of humanity seemed very far away from up here, and could very quickly be much closer.

He mulled over his life. Not much to show for his years on this planet. Matilda and he had raised five beautiful young ones, their lives were by far his most meaningful contribution. They had long since flown the coop, scattered to the four winds with rarely a visit. Still, he knew that each of them loved him and that helped some.

The rest of it wasn't so cheery. He had been born in this city, had spent all of his days fighting out a meager living. Every day seemed like a cock fight, trying desperately to get ahead among a flock of hundreds, thousands. Keeping bread on the table seemed like a full time job. In some ways the city seemed like a very large cage. He had never had time enough for the kids it seemed, and now that he did, they were gone. A tear rolled down Claddius' cheek as he sat on the ledge.

No one looked up at him. He was just another soul clinging to a ledge in the big city. It only became news if something more happened. Claddius had never been news, had never felt exceptional in any way. He had spent his days being led by others, turning this way or that because everyone else was turning this way or that. He knew that eventually he would have to face what he had come here to think through.

Matilda had clung bravely to life. She had never complained when times were bad and always celebrated when they could scrape up a little extra. Now she was gone. She had anchored his life and now she was gone. He reflected sadly on her lifeless body, lying before his imagination now just the way he found her a week ago. He always thought there would be a chance to say goodbye. Now he knew better. Life didn't always work like that.

With what seemed like remarkable clarity, Claddius came to a decision. Life had nothing further to offer him. He had tasted all of the crumbs that came his way and found most of them were bitter or spoiled. His chance to spread his wings and find some significance in his life were long gone. A young idealistic Claddius taunted him from within. "Look at you, you old fool! There's nothing left to live for!"

With a look of resignation, Claddius stepped to the front of the ledge and looked down. The milling traffic and midday bustle did not stop to see this moment in his life. With a sigh, Claddius leapt and flew to the park. Maybe the old guys brought day old muffins today, he thought.

The End

Erstwhile Heroics

Contemporary fiction by Dan Marvin

The fire whistle cut shrilly through the night air of Fire Wheel, Nebraska. It carried through the clear air to the ears of Fire Marshall Mark Adams just seconds before his pager picked up the insistent tone and ran with it as well. Hardly a nightly occurrence, the combination of siren and beeper had him out of bed before he was out of sleep and resulted in a groggy Fire Marshal Mark Adams sitting on the floor looking dazed for roughly 12 seconds.

He ran to the phone and called the station. The one line was busy. He cursed. Hustling to get his jacket before running into the night, Fire Marshal Mark Adams stopped to kiss Lucy, his wife, as she lay half awake in bed. "I will be back when I can, keep some coffee hot for me!" He yelled on his way out the door.

His 1986 Dodge started sluggishly in the 20 degree air. A pitiless moon gazed down on him and threw everyday items into the weird domain of the dead around him with improbable shadows and unlikely lines. Already, his keen olfactory senses had picked up a trace of smoke, it could be from a wood fire in Bill Keaning's house or it could be from a raging inferno threatening the life of someone in town. Mark knew everyone after 32 years in the same town, and he valued each and every one of them.

In Fire Wheel, nothing was far from anything else. His Dodge slid into the 'Fire Marshal' spot right outside the door and before the engine stopped spinning, he was out of it. He yanked the door to the station open with a bang and ran to the attendant. He saw three other firemen in various stages of dress and could hear the engines of at least another. "What's happening?" he shouted without formality.

"Parson Anderson's house is on fire" was the hurried reply. Without waiting for another word, he donned his protective clothing, mounted up a pumper crew, and started the siren. They swung onto Oak Street with a rush and headed out to the North end of town. Sure enough, the flames were illuminating the trees from 1/2 mile away, he knew this was a big one.

The night officer from the FWPD was already there, running around frantically trying to keep sightseers from interfering with the fire engines. "Is anyone in there?" shouted Fire Marshall Mark Adams. The shoulder shrug filled him with terror, he would have to go in and look. Parson Anderson had a 3 year old daughter and a five year old son living with him and Mark did not see them in the crowd.

The heat was intense, his nose dried out from the first inhalation even through the mask. He ran up the stairs that were already starting to burn and flew into room after room down the hall. The first was empty. In the second, rumpled bedding led him to check the bathroom. Kaitlin was inside, he grabbed her and covered her head in a wet towel. The next room was Sammy's but Sammy was not in it. Fire Marshall Mark Adams could not wait any longer,

107

he ran downstairs again and out into the night. The crash of the upstairs giving up followed him out the door and he put Kaitlin down as gently as he could with his heart thundering in his ears.

Next day's Fire Wheel Gazette showed a smiling Kaitlin Anderson perched on the back of her sooty father. Next to them was a concerned looking Fire Marshall Mark Adams. The caption underneath read 'Bosnia Turmoil Results in Bloodshed.' Editor Paul Mitchell looked at the caption, looked at the whirling printing press, and swore softly to himself.

The End

Phabulous Philosophy – Without houses and cars and windows and doors there would be little that would separate us from the animals. Literally.

Delusion of Mediocrity

Contemporary fiction by Dan Marvin

Way up on top of the cupboard, up almost further than he could reach, Jimmy's hand closed on a bit of paper and he pulled. The bit of paper became a bunch of paper and the bunch of paper soon cascaded onto the floor bringing its prize with it. It was wrong of his mother to hide his candy, Jimmy had already decided. Now he had to determine just what to do about it.

Jimmy sat on the floor of the family room, munching on the forbidden Tootsie Rolls and analytically assessed his situation. His mother was against him. She would not let him eat chocolate instead of vegetables, she would not let him run outside naked, and she forced him to go to school every morning at 8:15 AM. The terrible car propelled them closer and closer each morning until, sure enough, they arrived at J. Jason Seymore Wayward Boys Academy.

Headmaster Smith had learned his lesson the hard way. He had been against Jimmy from the beginning. One day Jimmy had hurt a little girl in his class and his teacher had sent him to see Headmaster Smith. Minutes later, the usually healthy principal was carried out on a stretcher and that was the last time he was seen at the Academy.

Jimmy's mouth curved upwards at the memory. He started to think about the possibilities for his mother. He was sure she suspected, the accidents that happened to people who crossed him were becoming harder and harder to write off as coincidences. The fact that she had gone through 8 boyfriends since the divorce also weighed heavily against him.

The chocolate covered face leered at his mother from the floor of the family room as she entered with his sneakers. A cold chill crept up her spine as she looked into his eyes. "Come on, Jimmy, time for school. Get your face wiped up!" Did she really think THAT was going to work? He began to concentrate. His mind started to slip into a dark, powerful place and...

"Jimmy, did you hear me? I said get ready!" His mom closed the window and dragged him to the bathroom for a cleanup. Jimmy sighed deeply. Someday. Someday he would find a way.

The End

Fabricated Factoid –
37% - percentage of US homes with alarm systems
64% - percentage of US homes with alarm system signs in the front yard

Two Things Everyone Wants but No One Has

A do-it-yourself guide to you by Dan Marvin

Pushing back from the table, young Jeremy McDaniel knew he was finished. The meal sat half ate before him but that wasn't it. He knew, deep down, that he could never again face his parents. The monkey on his back had grown too large. Resignedly, he packed his bags before they got home and pulled his Mustang out of the garage for the last time.

The street lights went by in a dizzying array as young Jeremy McDaniel tried to exorcise his demons through speed and a wanton disregard for human life, his own or anyone else's. When he ran out of road, he parked overlooking a large manmade lake, looking down a rocky embankment at the bleak gray day below.

Jeremy thought back to his first days at Iron Joe Academy for Gifted Boys, a special magnet school designed to teach him how to think and feel and act like a man instead of a boy. At first, it had gone well, his grades were good, he was well liked, he was happy. Slowly, all of that had eroded. Doubts nagged at the back of his mind. Was he good enough for Iron Joe's? He had cheated on a few tests and finally got caught. Instead of setting him on the right road, it sent him spiraling towards the abyss he now overlooked.

Ruck had seemed like a good guy at first, congenial, quick to laugh, good enough in classes to get by. Jeremy had started seeking him out more as his grasp on reality slowly slipped away. In time, Ruck was his friend but also his greatest challenge. The group that Ruck hung with were a mixture of good or bad, spending as much time thinking about girls as considering how to be better human beings.

Finally, it all broke down for Jeremy one day last month. He had been at a party at the house of one of Ruck's friends when he had been introduced to Cassandra. She was as beautiful as she was mysterious, he was quickly caught up in her web. The money he had been saving for college seemed to leap out of his pocket around her neck and down her throat. When his pockets were empty, she was on to greener pastures and he was finished.

All of these thoughts and more sped through his mind faster than he had sped through the California streets minutes ago. He couldn't face his parents, broke, failing out, and completely devoid of self confidence. The beckoning rocks below called to him. With grim determination, he clenched his jaw and made his decision. He bought a book called "How to get other people to look worse than you" by Dr. RC Bishop and read it cover to cover. In a matter of weeks, he was popular, self confident, and on his way to great riches.

The End

Sunset Harmony

A period piece by Dan Marvin

The wind chased itself across the rolling fields, stopping at this rock or that tree for a moment and then finding itself again, running laughing atop the sprigs of spring grass. It had been a hard winter, several of the cattle had perished for want of this grass that now grew so abundantly. Jane Diamond watched the tendrils of wind move through the hay but her eyes did not register the scene. They had a far off look that turned the clear blue of her irises into swimming pools of repressed desire.

It had been 14 months since Ned had ridden off and dropped off the face of the earth. Her inquiries at Wagonhead had been met with stoic indifference, he had neither been seen nor missed. Ned was a difficult man to love, she knew this intimately, and few would mark his passing with other than sympathy for the widow. Since then she and Jebediah had worked the land, grown the cattle, and kept a wary eye out for danger, whatever the form.

Occasionally Reverend Timmerman had stopped with kind words and some donations from the parishioners but most days were filled with windswept grass and work from sunup to sundown. Her hands had aged 50 years in 14 months and Jebediah was becoming as wild as the weeds in the hay. It was lonely but there were rewards. She cast a proud eye towards Jeb now as he ran with Shep the collie through the field.

"Mama, mama, there's a man headed this way!" The words stirred Jane to quick action. She gathered up the rifle, checked the load in the cylinder, and set it down next to her on the porch. It was telling that she also sent Jeb to the well to fetch water. She watched the swirl of dust that soon disgorged a man and his mount, a particularly unimpressive steed that looked powerful but half wild. The man showed similar traits.

"Evenin' Ma'am," he offered by way of greeting. "My horse is lame and I aint doing so hot myself, can I buy a meal and a night's sleep from you?" His question was met with the most thoughtful gaze he figured had ever been cast his way. He couldn't help but admire the curves behind the rifle.

"What's your name, cowboy?" was her question, he could hear the lilt of Irish that tinged her voice and he smiled.

"O'Grady, ma'am. Tiger O'Grady." He replied.

Her features softened a bit. "There's hay in the barn, Tiger O'Grady, and Jeb has brought up some water for you. You can sleep in the loft."

Tiger's smile lit up his whole face and Jane's resolve to send him packing at her earliest opportunity wavered a bit. "Thank you kindly, I'll go freshen up..."

… to be continued

Tune in next week for chapter II of *Sunset Harmony* the epic novel from Western legend Dan Marvin.

Sunset Harmony – Reprised

A period piece in several acts by Dan Marvin

Footsteps on the porch presaged the opening of the door and gave Jane time to reflexively fix her hair. The door let in some of the spring chill and Jane turned to see the broad shoulders of Tiger O'Grady filling the portal. His face was not handsome, rather it was intelligent but hard. A smile played at the corners of his eyes but did not translate itself to his mouth, not just yet. Jane straightened from the fire and addressed her guest, aware that her social skills had atrophied a bit on the lonely, windswept plains.

"There's stew on the fire, biscuits will be up in a minute, help yourself to both. Jeb, get Mr. O'Grady a plate down." Her eyes danced in the flames from the fire and his shone back with similar heat, drinking her in without seeming to do so. Jeb ran after the plate and was back in a moment, grinning from ear to ear. He stared at the stranger with eyes full of questions until his mother shooed him away.

"Thank you, Jeb," Tiger said, his manners as rusty as Jane's. "But you can both call me Tiger, just about everyone does and it don't sound normal to be called Mister."

"OK Tiger!" The enthusiasm in the youth's voice was infectious. "Do you want to see the elk jaw I found?" Tiger and Jeb conferred together for a few moments, admiring the trophy until Jane interjected.

"Jeb, you leave Tiger be, he must be famished. Come on up to the table and sit a spell, Tiger O'Grady, this day will end a little more peaceably than yesterday if I'm any judge of horses, or men. When you're ready, I'd be powerful interested in any news you might have for us. Her eyes mirrored her son's.

Tiger O'Grady's full attention was devoted to his meal, he downed two bowls of stew and three biscuits before he paused for even a minute. Finally, another bowl later he said "Ma'am, that's some mighty fine cooking and I'm much obliged for your kindness. I'm pretty new to these parts and don't have much news as such but what I do know I'll tell ya. You wouldn't be looking for a spare hand would you?"

These three sentences seemed to be all he was capable of for now as Tiger crossed his arms and leaned back against the wall. "We don't know much about you, Mr. O'Grady," Jane said cautiously.

"Well, let me tell you a little then," Tiger began...

Tune in next time for part three of the series, coming to bookstores everywhere just as soon as they realize what fools they've been not to sign me to a multi-book contract

Celluloidsitosis

Contemporary fiction by Dan Marvin

Two rows down the young couple clung together like otters, playfully tugging and grasping each other as Howard looked on in disgust. For 18 years he had frequented the Starscape Theatre and each year the behavior of the young patrons had gotten worse. At one time Howard was filled with optimism that he would eventually find someone that wanted to cuddle with him in the movie house but the last several years had showed him that life was often cruel and rarely smiled on those of superior intelligence.

He watched as the young lovers held hands, oblivious to the needs of moviegoers like himself who demanded an environment devoid of distraction. Often he came to the 2:30 matinees, frequented only by preteens and social deviants. He flattered himself into thinking that he broke the stereotype. Tonight had been different, he needed people, wanted to be among others of his phylum and sought his first love, the movies.

Eventually the boy and his date lessened in importance, they settled in to watch the show, his arm flung around her shoulder in careless possessiveness that Howard envied. The characters onscreen seemed a little less lifelike tonight, more like actors paid to portray their parts than inhabitants of Howard's little universe. Usually he could immerse himself in the drama unfolding but tonight he seemed aware only of the aching in his heart, longing for someone to share his outlook on life, to laugh at his jokes. Howard's mouth set into a thin line as he stared at the screen.

The THX sound system hammered the dramatic points home, he wished for the first time that the sound was more subtle and did not involve him so personally. The action raced towards him, seeking to involve him emotionally with the characters on the screen. Instead, he felt his mind uncharacteristically drifting towards his own life, the action on the screen meant no more than the motions of persons he would never know caught in situations he could not fathom.

Finally, at last, the lights came up. Howard sat for awhile among the popcorn containers and empty beverage cups, watching the young couple in front of him. Secretly he hated them because they represented all that was not present in his life. They eventually stood and his eyes followed them over 14 seats and they walked in front of... her. She was completely black and white, no red, blue, or yellow to mar her beauty. She sat with her back to Howard but he knew immediately that she was a soulmate.

He almost stumbled as he walked four rows ahead. "My name is Howard," he began. "Would you like to go to a movie with me sometime?"

The End

The Craven Blunderbuss

Fiction in response to your votes by Dan Marvin

The doctors said I wasn't short enough to be a midget but damn it, I FELT short enough. My tiny little legs barely dragged on the floor when I sat in a 'big people's' chair. It was tough to look sexy in Geranimals and who was going to date me anyway? My life was spent with a big chip on one shoulder and women's purses bumping into the other.

After one particularly humiliating day in my job as a refiller of bathroom condom dispensers (one more unstable toilet seat and I was going to invest in some hip waders), I walked glumly along North Terrace Way on my way back to South Upton when I heard a small "Pssst" emanating from the alley to my left. Expecting rotting fruit would soon be following the expulsion of air, I cringed as I looked towards the source of the sound.

Instead of youthful miscreants, I found myself looking straight into the loveliest pair of eyes I had ever seen. Although the benefit of being my height was the ability to stare at most women's breasts as a matter of course, it was more disconcerting to see eyes the color of a stormy sea sky staring back without blinking. "Hello" I began uncertainly.

Her name was Therese and she explained the organization for which she worked. There were hundreds of people just like me, she explained, that felt much of the same anger with the world that I feel. They maintained a house where they could congregate, rant, rave, commune, drink, eat, and enjoy each other's company. There was also a factory designed specifically to produce items for small people by small people. I was entranced.

My first day on my new job was exciting. All of the equipment was my size. My boss was a man named Gerald who towered an intimidating 4'9". He gently explained to me the operation of the equipment. I was to be seated inside a control area and direct the movements of some high tech looking equipment from there. I quickly assented to learning the controls and stepped into the small cabin.

Gerald turned some levers and grinned at Therese. The water began to rise in the 'control cabin' and I started to panic. It finally dawned on me as the last respirable air made its way down my lungs followed by unbreathable fluid that I wasn't the only almost midget with a chip on his shoulder.

The End

What time doth mete

Vague memories of the present by Dan Marvin

The hard packed dirt wandered its way through ill-kempt fescue, leading from the ancient driveway to the equally aged house. It had been many years since a lawnmower had been this way and longer still since children's feet had found joy in the treasures beneath the grass. Beneath a bush, a rusty wheel of a toy bulldozer which had long since given up trying to plow the root filled soil is the only evidence that once little boys had whiled away carefree summer hours here.

The brook still babbles where it always did but its neatly contained path now meanders back and forth through cat tails and brushy trees. No cows contentedly munch the saplings to keep them in check anymore. The water skippers still dance in water that smells of wild wintergreen and silver darts of minnows chasing the bugs would still attract attention if anyone was there to notice.

A nest of bees would quickly deter anyone from sitting on the chaise lounge on the porch, their rule is not contested and they use the cushions that once had held laughing family members to build their nest. Swallows fly freely into the corners just like they always have but the paint is peeling from the black iron now and the roof above will not give shelter for much longer. The steps that would enter into the kitchen are still solid but the floor they led into is not.

Inside the farmhouse is a gallery of forgotten memories. The scuffed linoleum still holds the kitchen floor together where generations of Matchbox cars had rolled freely each Christmas and crumbs of birthday cakes long gone collected in the corners. The smell of dark corners and unused canning jars wafts up from the cellar door, left open by some thrill seeker or animal looking for shelter from the rain. The living room still has the lingering odor of cigarette smoke and the echo of thank yous for knitted socks and mittens, toys bought at Lindgrens for the kids, and needles of hemlock trees cut from the woods above.

The outside is encroaching into the house, a strong maple has gained a foothold through the front porch which had been none too sturdy even when it was used and its leafy green has pushed through the living room window, broken when a bird collided with it three summers ago. The rushing wind and running water could be heard distinctly here if there was anyone to hear it. The time worn stairs have held up a little better, they would still lead the weary foot to the floor above. To the right would be the playroom, the huge round oak table still dominating the scene but threatening to fall into the living room now.

Straight ahead is the closet, the one that had always been full of puzzles and saved egg cartons and a little dab of thread if you needed it, the closet that had the entrance to the attic for a roof, the closet that you only went into if Grandma was with you and not at all in later years. Down the hall is the room you always stayed in, the bed no longer there but memories of a burning 60 watt bulb on a cold winters' night and the television wafting up the stairs still fresh.

Down the hall is the room that used to be your moms but now belongs to the swallows that found the open window and moved right in. Bits of nest and droppings are the only furnishings now but listening close might bring back the sound of music boxes and the smell of cedar chests and you can still make out the pattern on the floor if you look close enough. Around the corner is the guest room, the one that grownups used when they stayed over. Now it's a maze of cobwebs and old leaves but once it held the nicest bed and the prettiest covers. The smell of an animals den would make the weary visitor reluctant to enter now.

Outside, just over the brook, the woods have started to relentlessly retake the fields that had taken years to clear. The greenery still hides bear and deer tracks and a whistle can still startle woodchucks into sitting up and answering. Somewhere out there is the old gas well and grown over logging roads. Soon, no trace of man's intrusion will scar this wild land.

The bridge that Grandpa built when he was still alive is precarious now, no car would drive across it willingly and it keeps this house and its memories safe from the outside world. The sound of a car out on the nameless county road floats through the still summer air but no ear is there to hear it.

The End

Author's Note – I don't think the farm really looks like this, the last report I had suggested that a nice young couple had bought it at the auction and were keeping it in fine repair and loving it as it had been loved for generations. Still, in my mind's eye this is how it looks, frozen forever as the life that once dwelled there slowly closed up camp, moved away, or lost track of the time.

A Casual Disrespect for Authority

Contemporary fiction by Dan Marvin

The rhythmic pulses of his CRT updating had John in a slightly mind-numb state when his boss rounded the corner to his cubicle and startled him. He was slightly worried about getting fired from his third job in four months but not so worried that he actually did anything about it. "John," his boss began "I'm having a problem getting the D9 inks fully dilute and I can't use any more solvent, any ideas?"

"Ahhhh" John responded and then quickly lost interest. He wandered over to the water cooler to get a drink to buy himself more time. The water spattered as it came out of the device and the ink on his page began to run.

"Of course! Why didn't I think of that?" his boss asked and ran out to implement John's idea of using water to dilute the inks. John was still in a daze a month later when he was promoted to his boss' job who was promoted to Vice President. A knock came at his door.

"John, what do you make of these press clippings stating that the Theta project just won't fly?" the President of the company asked.

"Ahhhh" John replied and went to wrinkle up the letter he was writing to his girlfriend on company time. Instead, he inadvertently grabbed the clippings in question and threw them into the garbage can.

"You're right! All the research bears it out! We can't let the press dictate corporate policy. Thanks for your blunt assessment, most men would have tried to find out what I thought and repeated it back to me." the President concluded. A week later, John was VP of Market Research.

"I've been thinking John" the chairman of the board began "that we need to do something to boost our market share in the soft drink segment. We need an ad campaign that's simple and direct. What do you think?"

"Ahhhh..." John began. The Chairman looked at him for a moment and said "That's perfect! Just that. We don't need a lot of words, just a sigh of satisfaction! Brilliant!" A week later, John was President of the company.

John sat twiddling his thumbs one day and wondering just how he had gotten to be President of Amalgamated Industries Corp when a glittering light caught his attention from the building across the way. He opened the window and leaned way out to see what it was when he lost his balance and plummeted towards the ground.

"Ahhhhh!!!" John screamed as he fell 30 stories. From floor after floor could be heard mutterings of "phenomenal... perfect... just what we need!"

The End

The Hesitant Woodsmen

Contemporary fiction by Dan Marvin

Wrapped tightly in the fog like a cocoon, Wispy Willow slept a light happy sleep. She dreamed of waving gently in a summer breeze, bird bedecked branches bustling busily as swarms of swallows sang and twittered. If she had had lips, they would have crept ever so slightly upwards in the corners with the memory. As it was, she pumped sap with a contented rhythm.

Elmer Elm listened to the constant cacophony of Wispy's happy sap and shuddered to himself in disgust. He had been around long enough to know that all was not right in the enchanted woods. If he had lungs, he would have called out to Wispy to keep that claptrap to herself lest she rouse an angry spirit. Deep down, he just wished that he could sleep more himself. After 170 years in the same place, sleep came hesitantly or not at all.

The bright sun finally poked from beneath a veil of clouds and greeted the trees. Wispy turned her branches towards him and even Elmer felt a little better as the photosynthesized sugars reached his roots for storage. Maybe the evil he had been sensing was just in his head, the fantasies of an old tree. Maybe there was only good in this w.... wait, what was that?

A rumbling rent the still morning air like a shotgun blast. It was the backfire of an old truck, lumbering its way up the mountain. What could this turn of events mean, wondered Elmer? Soon he had his answer, two men parked the truck in his shady glen and looked eagerly around them. They saw an orange wisp of plastic on Wispy's trunk and began to unpack.

"BZZZZZZ" went the angry sound of the chainsaw as the men limbered it up. They topped it with fuel/oil mixture and revved it, then advanced on Wispy. Elmer could feel her terror communicated through the ground like shock waves. No, this couldn't be happening! He really hadn't wanted her killed for keeping him up! The other trees looked at him reproachfully, surely they couldn't think he had anything to do with this?

The saw began to clear scrub brush from around Wispy's base. As the men advanced on her, another truck drove into sight. The man inside beckoned frantically to get their attention. He shouted and pointed and all three jumped into their vehicles and sped away. "Whew!" thought Elmer, "what a narrow escape!"

Wispy gradually calmed and Elmer grew warm with the fact that she was safe. In fact, he was growing VERY warm. He looked at the sun and was surprised to see it almost obscured in something, not a cloud exactly. Was that smoke he smelled? Elmer began to think that perhaps this was a very bad day indeed.

The End

Seven Farsacs from Redemption

Science and Sorcery from Dan Marvin

Dr. Antulpac Quintain slung two saddlebags of Detherium alloy over his Zwarth and spurred the steed into action. It was true that the glider was faster and had a farther range, but the glider's tracking device should even now be sending the Overlord Enforcement battalions to the Smith continent on the far end of Devon II and he needed all the time he could get. The Zwarth would work well in the valleys and might be overlooked by the satellites.

The multipoedia of the Zwarth's ungainly design were wonderful for crossing rocky country but lousy at dust control, Quintain's eyes soon burned from the ash laden particulates that found homes there. He wished he had brought goggles, a drink, so many things but there had been no time. In all he had mustered 8 glorious centiticks of time to pluck the Detherium from the momentarily confused security hatch, push it into saddlebags, and throw his two parcels onto his getaway creature. If his estimations were correct, the Abstention sect would pay mightily for the bomb grade ore and he could stow away in a slow freighter to an exotic port and get off of this God forsaken rock.

Quintain's eyes narrowed as he followed the ravine to the jumble of rocks below. His steadily plodding mount did not seem agitated but there was motion ahead and his pulse started to quicken. He pulled out a phase disruptor, set it on the highest setting, and kicked his already overworked mount just a little harder. The beast reared up a couple of inches but otherwise continued at about the same pace on about the same trajectory. Quintain cursed. His glider was probably getting ready to crash into the Sea of Abathee now, out of fuel. He hoped that the sacrifice was worth it.

At command Central, Lieutenant Depathno leered into his infrared tracking scope and watched the Zwarth crawl along the canyon path. They had seen Dr. Quintains glider scoot away twenty decaticks ago and followed it curiously for a few ticks until he thought to activate the computer override. It was congenial enough to tell him that the Master was not in presently but that it would love to take a message. He sent the self destruct signal and watched on satellite telemetry as the glider crashed into a mountain.

Now, the Zwarth was locked in his sites and the pesky treason of Dr. Antulpac Quintain was about to be a short-lived abomination. His finger hovered over the button and then he struck venomously. A bolt of blinding radiation came out of the sky and struck the animal, obliterating it. Depathno chuckled to himself.

On the ground, Quintain quickly averted his eyes when the laser blast erupted in front of him. He watched as his recent boss struggled atop the Zwarth 20 paces before him and then suddenly evaporated. So far his plan was working, only two farsacs to go...

The End

Amoeba Playground

Contemporary fiction by Dan Marvin

The water droplet sat poised, ready for the leap. With just a little more mass, it thought that it could finally fulfill its destiny and return to the water table. The day had started out slow, riding high above the landscape, an indistinguishable denizen of a plump, moisture laden cloud. At first, the droplet had been cold, very cold. When gravity could no longer be denied, it abandoned ship and headed to the great unknown below.

The ground had come up to meet it at a blinding pace, its gray, dreary world retreated and was quickly replaced with green and brown. The droplets' brothers and sisters cascaded down with it, each of them hopeful that they would end up on porous soil and not in a discarded McDonald's coffee cup as a mosquito breeding ground.

A particular piece of the greenery had claimed the droplet, it shed some of its molecules in a satisfying 'splat' and waited for gravity to help it continue its journey. With very little by way of motivational energy, it sat gently vibrating with Brownian motion waiting for enough of its kin to help it gain sufficient mass to head to the earth. Another droplet joined it, a third lent some matter and the droplet began to roll down the leaf. It was a halting journey, interspersed with occasional stops as it gained potential energy and waited to convert it to kinetic.

Now, it sat expectantly on the very end of the leaf, restrained by a small ridge created by a hungry insect with no concern for wayward water droplets, only its ever expanding gullet. Surely a few more splatters would help send it to its final resting place! The clouds had begun to break up, the rain was fitful now and far from constant. There was a even a hint of the dreaded sun, peaking through the edge of the clouds, wanting nothing more than to evaporate a poor, unfulfilled water droplet and make it take its journey all over again.

Just as the droplet began to resign itself to evaporation, a glorious thing happened. A small puff of wind happened by, perhaps sent by the guardian of water droplets or maybe just an errant puff looking for an excuse to show off. Whatever the source, the leaf tipped a bit and the water droplet slid off. It tumbled downward quickly, taking on a bottom heavy look that made it aerodynamic. This was it! The droplet was finally going to return to the earth!

Expecting to hit the ground fast, the droplet was surprised to find itself integrated into a larger body of water. It looked around at all the other molecules for a brief instant and then lost its identity as an individual droplet. As its conscience merged with the whole, it was vaguely aware of the Styrofoam surrounding it, the stale remnants of age old coffee. It would take a miracle to make the water table from here. The droplet ceased to be.

The End

The Ransom Trail

Contemporary fiction by Dan Marvin

The swirling dervish of dust settled on the jackets of the cow punchers. They had long since given up trying to brush it off and settled on keeping their heads down almost as low as their spirits. It had been a long, brutal drive; the cattle had dwindled from almost 1200 head to less than 700. Water had been sparse and forage spotty. Their meager supplies had lasted only 3/4 of the way to Durango, now they were living on jackrabbits and whatever they could forage from the range.

The dusty wagon pulled up next to a pond of brackish water and Cookie called out to the crew "Dinner in 30 minutes, get washed up, hee hee hee!" Johnny Silas didn't find the joke too funny, there wasn't enough water in the hole to let all of the cattle have a short drink, say nothing about getting washed up. He stopped his mount and ground hitched it onto a patch of likely looking grass. Later, he would let it loose, it wouldn't wander from the water hole.

His saddle and saddlebags were thrown on the ground and his rifle leaned against them. He looked at his meager possessions with disgust, he had been riding the range for 16 years and this was what he had to show for it. A horse that wasn't his, and a saddle that had seen better days. If he wasn't dog tired from the trail, he would get out his bottle of whiskey and chase away his blues. Hell, maybe he'd do that anyway.

The thought quickly went out of his head when Cookie rang the chow bell. He was second in line after Sam McGraw, somehow Sam had a sixth sense when it came to food. The rabbit stew was filling, that was about all he could say for it. Johnny took some salt out of his pack and sprinkled it on, it made the stringy meat palatable at least.

The halfhearted tales around the campfire that night involved women who would and women who almost did, gunfights that might have been and futures that most certainly lay in Durango when the rest of these cattle were delivered. It would only be three days now, Johnny thought he should feel some excitement but all he felt was hollow. When they sold the cows, the trail boss would count out 3 gold coins, hand them to Johnny, and tell him goodbye. This was the last run of cattle for the 3BarF brand, after that he was on his own. He hoped that maybe they would let him keep the horse he had been riding since it wouldn't be needed. Most likely they would sell that too.

A wild war whoop exploded from the night and gunshots rang out, then nothing. The whole encampment had guns out and ears cocked but all that could be heard was far off hooves on the hard packed earth. Comanches had swooped in and run off over 100 head they would find in the morning. After his watch was over, Johnny took out the bottle of whiskey.

The End

A Buoyant Moment

The frazzled assistant DA looked distractedly towards the door, looked back at his papers, and then jerked his head back up with a slack jaw as J. Nelson Jones strolled into the courtroom like he owned the place. The young man's hand went involuntarily to his forehead as if to say "what did I do to deserve this?"

The defendant leered his way to his chair, dressed in chains and an orange jumpsuit but looking for all the world like he had just come from the salon. Squeaky Matziano was no stranger to America's court rooms and was almost as cocky as his defense lawyer.

It had been two months since Judge Spenser had been killed and this was the first time the prosecutor had even sat in the same room with the defendant and his counsel. The judge's neatly strangled body had divulged little, the lake it had ultimately floated out of had produced even less. Matziano had the motive, the opportunity - and the upper hand. With no witnesses and an alibi sticking to her story, it looked to be an uphill battle for the DA's department.

Kent Lariman knew why he had been assigned to this case. He was experienced enough to be considered capable but expendable enough to make a fine scapegoat when the case crashed in flames. For him, his career hung in the balance and he knew it. His boss was not unfair, not unhelpful, and not unpolitical.

Nancy Dumont, the judge in the case, called the court to order with a businesslike brusqueness that Kent was used to. "Mr. Lariman, you speak for the DA's office, do you not?"

"I do your honor." At the moment, Kent spoke only for Kent.

"Mr. Jones insists that this case be thrown out for lack of evidence. At the moment, I am inclined to agree with him. What can you say to sway me?" Judge Dumont had no time to waste words.

"I can prove that the defendant had the inclination to murder Justice Spenser, that he has committed murders before, and that he was near the area that it happened. I am confident his alibi will not hold water. I request that Your Honor give us the opportunity to collect more facts and present them to a jury." Kent knew not to waste time with Legalese.

"And how does the defendant reply?" Judge Dumont inquired.

"My client has been the victim of a mean spirited attack upon his honor at the hands of the DA's office, your honor!" J. Nelson Jones was beginning to get warmed up and he was definitely in his element. "If he is guilty, may God strike him down!"

In an unfortunate choice of words, Squeaky Matziano's counsel sentenced him to damnation. A blinding flash illuminated the courtroom and the smoldering remains of his client graced the chair next to J. Nelson Jones. A thunderclap punctuated the sentence.

"I believe, Your Honor, that the defendant would like to change his plea to guilty."

Conclusion – Well, there you have it! You probably want some history, right? I started tagging my stories with "contemporary fiction by Dan Marvin" in college and so I just left it in there for most of them. Some I had to take out due to space on the page because I knew you were a savvy consumer and wouldn't want a lot of pages with just one line. The things I do for you!

You'll no doubt be happy to note that *A Change of Briefs for the Reading Room* is already underway. Check back often for this exciting next chapter in the *Briefs* series. There will be twice the thrills, twice the chills, and twice the excitement! But probably about the same number of pages.

If you're reading this part, you must still have a few minutes left before you're done. I'll do what I can to fill them but I'll be honest, I don't have a lot left. That was a lot of writing! Don't worry, there's more where they came from and honestly, if you stick this in a drawer and pull it out again in a few months, you won't remember many of them. It will be like having a brand new book. I hope you enjoyed these micro-novels and thank whoever bought you this book for their generosity. See you soon!

- Dan Marvin 2008

Notes:

Groceries:

List of People to Give Copies of *Briefs:*